THE

DOG

WANTER

To my life-partner Charlie also my writing buddy.

To my gems. Maddy and Roly and our friends:
SWEET thoughts to all.

>
> Thanks to LINDA and STELLA.

Suspend a little belief and I hope you find it an easy read.

Chapter 1
Nancy Meets Percy

In she blew that cold February afternoon. Eyeing **all**.

Around them she prowled before sliding into a seat and splaying wide her legs. Her gaze was forward. Reader, those eyes of hers! Blue-green and sparkling as brightly as does a Mediterranean sea-surface when the sun beats down to form a thousand cutting mirrors.

This girl could slit her eyes. Pin you. Arrest and penetrate.

Her heart-shaped face was home to even features. Her hair was russet-red.

The class teacher Miss McBride who happened to be recovering from a personal matter, was taken by surprise by this unexpected entrant. She moved over to Nancy, board-marker still in hand.

Nancy stood up, "My mother said you were expecting me. I couldn't wait until tomorrow to meet you all. So, I let myself in," Nancy added shrugging her shoulders.

The classroom rustled. Pupils sat forward in their chairs. The young teacher welcomed Nancy and hurried back to the front of the class to conclude the day's lesson.

Later that evening Miss McBride recanted the event to her partner.
"She just blasted in... like Mary Poppins. And the way she sat, Harvey...like a French Bulldog lain out on a marble floor...took a swig of her water. It was as if she was sucking *limonada and coconut* through a bamboo straw. Eyes like a cat."

That was not all Miss McBride wanted to say to her live-in lover of six years; the early one's fun-soaked and heady.

But I digress...let me take you back, reader, to the **very** first meeting of Nancy and Percy but before that I must introduce to you another character in our story, Mrs Truffit.

Mrs Truffit, the headteacher of Langton Green Primary school, was rarely seen during the school hours but came out of her office every day at

3.35pm as precisely as a figurine in a cuckoo clock. Thus, handily missing all the hullaballo of home-time with its high spirits and belongings-collecting. She avoided that wall of parents and care-givers, too.

She'd appear, a woman of some size, exuding expertise and experience, immaculately dressed in a series of tailored suits that were sometimes checked and sometimes grey but always stylish.

Broaching the playground in all weathers with her hands clasped either behind her back, or out in front of her in a sort of praying position. She'd unclasp them and wave to the backs of the one hundred and thirty children in her care, taking a mild avuncular interest in the stragglers.

This particular afternoon was no different. She spotted Percy Baskerville for the second-time that week standing unclaimed in the centre. There he remained without complaint until the playground drained.

He was on the small side for his age with longish, rather straggly mid-brown hair. He had an open face and lovely round eyes like an owl's, all-knowing.

"Ah Master Baskerville… Late again are they?" the Head said warmly.

She and he were on good terms. Mrs Truffit enjoyed his outlook. The affable young fellow would ask searching questions, listen, and then make pertinent points.

From her corner Nancy watched the two of them. Though she had never met Mrs Truffit she sensed a good-humoured woman but knew even the most benign figures, when at risk, could turn nasty on the turn of a coin. She needed to get out of the playground without detection. This Mrs Truffit if in danger of being caught skipping correct procedure might cartwheel into some governing nightmare. Bear down on her from above or beneath, funneling fury and materialise in embarrassing phone calls or even confinement. An ice-cold blast bore through Nancy on that February afternoon as she prayed she wouldn't be caught.

It was then that Percy caught sight of Nancy, up against the wall. With the slightest rounding of his eyes he acknowledged her plight. Mrs Truffit was suggesting they waited in her office.

"You do know Year 6 ARE allowed to make their own way home," Nancy could hear her say to her chest high companion. "Can't you get your mother to e-mail a retraction? You're eleven…and one of our more mature pupils."

Percy shrugged, "I've tried. She has views."
For a moment Nancy thought the game was up but just as Mrs Trufitt was about to spot her, crouching in the corner, there was a call from Percy's dad.

Nancy broke cover and almost running somehow by stealth, skill or pure magic slid out of school behind Percy without detection and once on the other side of the school gate Nancy immediately positioned herself before Mr Baskerville with his dangling keys and his desire to get home.

"Mr Baskerville, I presume. I'm Nancy Renard. I'm new. Could you please take me home? My mother has been delayed by the capitalist system and the Artic Vortex threatens snow."

Percy stood and looked as if he would not get in the car without her. His father, prey to indecision at the best of times watched him shake his head in solidarity. Overcoming his initial reluctance, Mr Baskerville barely hesitated before saying, "Jump in."

By the time they reached Nancy's which was only around the corner from his own house, Mr Baskerville had heard a good deal about Nancy and he knew how much she wanted a dog.

Chapter 2
23 Lavender Gardens

Nancy was much taken by her new home. For one thing, she delighted in the natural beauty of its surrounding which was a canvas of gentle green with hills that sloped upwards from the flat, easy, well-mown grass of the village centre, perfectly parted by a merry brook. For another thing, it was good to see her mother happy.

"This village is not too big and not too small…Not on the rat track," Nancy's mother, Fern, told a neighbour as she turned the key. And three bedrooms, too!" she'd added.

At school Nancy was fast taken up by the "in" crowd becoming an integral part of their dance routine by Monday lunch. She'd picked up the steps with the ease of a Cuban salsa dancer. By Tuesday, she'd encouraged a few changes adding a row of cartwheels and an impressive backflip. On Friday, the girls delivered a sensational display in assembly to rapt applause. Their faces beamed.

That wasn't her only success. Nancy had a natural passion for science. She had acquired her numberbonds by age five and went through maths books like a bullet. She devoured them not in bite sized chunks but gulped them down. It caused problems. Many a good teacher staggered under the strain of this voracious appetite. Sweated overtime, sourcing new material. Indeed, became close to tears until Nancy devised a system where she self-marked her work and copied them in.

She enjoyed untangling things. The exploration of figures was a joy and she could get a grip of even the most stubborn problems. There was not much above and beyond Nancy when it came to mathematics.

Quite used to outpacing the class, she didn't mind helping others and did this rather successfully. Those challenged by algebraic principles, well, she somehow managed to remove the scales from their eyes. You could see the enlightenment slowly appear on their faces as, one after the other, they would smile and declare, "Yes I get it!"

It was as if she was producing binoculars and pointing them in the direction of a Peregrine

Falcons nest. At first, there was a time each child felt confusion, a blurriness and then a thrilling sighting together with a feeling of self-satisfaction and belonging.

She had such a knack for getting novel concepts across. Noah Taylor who after such a Nancy pep talk gave up his rapid wild guessing (three and seventeen are twenty-four!) and went home determined to drill his number-bonds into his head somehow.
"She could be on Countdown," he said to his mother with a sigh and allowed himself to be signed up to Kumon.

One tricky incident had marred Nancy's almost clean transference to the school. She had been approached by Miss Trotts, the games teacher, who'd noticed during netball class what a natural talent Nancy had for shooting goals. It didn't seem to matter where the girl stood, she got them in. Amazed by this accuracy Miss Trott's was further struck by Nancy's extraordinary foot work.

Langton Green happened to be a goal attack down and with a forthcoming match looming (with Miss Trott's nemesis Mrs Archer and her hotshot lot from Wyre Piddle) Miss Trott thought her prayers had been answered. But Nancy refused to play and said she was unavailable weekends. When Miss Trott's pressed her for the reason why, Nancy was forced to create a fanciful story about being a carer for her mother who had some mysterious debilitating virus.

One day Fern ran to the school gates in a grey singlet waving her arms and seizing up Nancy with great affection. Miss Trott was perplexed as the two ran off together giving a vibrant sense of healthy body tissue. Henceforth, Miss Trott was more determined than ever to keep her Riboflavins in order.

You might have imagined Nancy to be thrilled with the success of her first weeks at school but Nancy had a hole. And this hole without the sticking plaster of school routine on the Monday morning of half-term, split into a gaping one… fish out of water stuff… and it showed no signs of healing.

Years of accumulated "want" had built up within her. Each new time the rumbling, foaming desire grew stronger. Now it would well up like a geezer, threatening to break forth out of her mouth and torrent on her world.

She called down on an iron will to stifle it – imagining herself to be a pot of soup on the hob, understanding when reaching boiling she only had to remove herself from the kitchen and wait for it to subside.

"I'm going for a walk," she'd say over her shoulder and set off down the garden path. Out of harm's way so her mother could enjoy the novelty of home ownership and her pink marble effect shower splash-back.

Off to wear herself out on a mini excursion hoping exercise might reset her moral compass. Or perhaps some mishap or wonder might distract her. There were always the dogs to see. She'd pass them with lingering eyes.

This particular morning, she was passed by on the lane by horse riders. Nancy froze to the spot as a young girl, no older than herself, rode past her on the most beautiful piebald pony, accompanied by a gorgeous leggy, fox-eared yellow dog, unleashed by the girl's side.

Then some distance on strode out a dancing elegant war horse, large and chestnut. The immaculate woman upon it, sat high up in the saddle.

Nancy stood right back on the grass verge. She fixed first on the pony, then the girl… horse… woman and then the dog. Nancy's eyes drank up the sight, inflaming her, and fixed them into a lurid green stare.

Outwardly smiling Nancy gestured a token of appreciation. The woman gave the slightest nod of her head, gathered her reins, squeezed her thighs and jogged past in a blaze of bronze glory.

That night in bed Nancy relived this brief encounter. The yellow dog was everything she'd dreamed of. Insomnia burrowed into her, setting her alight, and there she lay on burning coals, her old desire emerging fresh and unforgiving.
To counteract this sleeplessness, she counted dogs not sheep:
Yellow dog
Great Dane
Cockerpoo

Akita
Saluki
Pharaoh Hound
Labradoodle
Cairn Terrier
Border Terrier
Golden Retriever
West Highland
Chihuahua
Mexican Hairless
Bloodhound
Scottie
Boxer
French Bull dog
Otter hound

That night weird dog-shaped shadows appeared on the walls of her new bedroom. Exhausted and tormented, not knowing whether to keep her eyes wide open or tightly shut, she kept on with her list, now mixing up the breeds imagining her own special cross.

She'd fight fire with fire. She's have it out with her mother. Nancy Renard must have a dog.

Chapter 3
Percy and Nancy

We next find Nancy at home in the kitchen pouring out *Frosties,* with an egg on the boil. On the dot of eleven she delivered a tray to her mother. A smooth-shelled, softly boiled egg sat in a much-loved tiger eggcup (handmade by Fern and gifted to Nancy) on a tray alongside a generous pile of buttered soliders, orange juice, coffee, extra toast with butter, marmite and marmalade. Flower in a vase, the lot.

Near noon, Fern surfaced. She was freshly showered and feeling as light as a feather. For a moment Nancy wondered if she could keep her mouth shut another week. But the night before had scared her. It was as if someone had taken the top of her head off, like a knife through the top of the shell of the soft-boiled egg, poked a large stick in and stirred. Stuck it down through her neck slushing her guts, puncturing them. Letting out all the air.

"What colour shall we paint the living room?" her mother gayly asked. "What is it with English people with all this magnolia?"

"How about Yellow? or Saffron... Mum my behaviour since we moved has been exemplary," said Nancy.
Fern sensed it coming.
"You've bought the house..." continued Nancy moving towards her.
"It's the last thing I think about at night and the FIRST thing I think about in the morning,"
"But Nancy...we've only just got here," Fern said the smile falling from her face.
"A puppy, mum...a puppy...with an ever-wagging tail?" said Nancy.
"What about a hamster?" responded Fern with conviction.
"A puppy," blurted Nancy "The heart wants what the heart wants!"
"But Nancy...we can't afford a dog. We're out all day," said Fern.
"I don't care about money. About heating or food!" Nancy implored. "You **said** when we got our own house I could have a dog!"
"But that was before interest rates went up," said Fern "And there would be dog sitters and vet's bills!"
"Fix your rates Mum. Get insurance. I'll sort the sitter!" Nancy said.

Fern couldn't think what to say and mumbled a "We'll see."

"We'll see, we'll see!" laughed Nancy in exasperation. "Words not Deeds!" she shouted although she didn't slam the kitchen door she didn't close it quietly either.

Oh, why couldn't she have a dog? Her mother so flexible and accommodating in other things. Why so rigid on this? The only thing she really cared about. The current situation seemed impossible.

Nancy stomped up the stairs, hurled herself on the bed and kicked her legs back and forth as she sat there. Then she sprung up, burst out of her bedroom, went back down the stairs into the kitchen. She was barely an inch away from her mother's face. "Tik Tok," she threatened and left through the back door, this time slamming it so hard it shook in its hinges.

It was a stroke of good fortune that very soon after this turbulent exit, Nancy encountered Percy who too was taking a breather from the impositions of family life. He had spent the whole morning with his rapacious little sister Ada whilst his parents enjoyed adult time before the Sunday Roast at two.

"I suppose it's a change from the National Trust," he confided good-humouredly.
Nancy was struck at how calm he was.

There, on the village green, the two of them stood. Nancy, taller, bent her head as she uncorked herself and together they began to walk along the brook.
"Ever since I can remember…since I was six…it's been *we'll see, we'll see…*" she said.
Percy said nothing but kept on listening.
"It was my sixth birthday I think or seventh…mum had been acting strangely. All excited. Did a countdown…fourteen, thirteen, twelve…you know what I mean. She was wired."

The young pair were now sat upon the old log just off the village green on the footpath. Percy sat by her side with his head slightly inclined.
"And when I awoke," recalled Nancy, "on the morning of my birthday there was this weight at the bottom of my bed. My heart took a leap. I switched the light on but instead of a puppy I saw this metallic paper all gathered at the top in a bow of white ribbon. I knew instantaneously this package was no living thing. My heart dropped

like a stone. Well… it fell out of me really," confessed Nancy swinging her legs back and forth. And Percy didn't contradict her.

"Mum burst in as I was unwrapping the present. It was a life-size statue of a setter. *Look darling*, mum said, *"It's a dalmation!"*

Percy who'd met Fern felt he could picture the scene.

"What did you say?" he asked.

"Thanks, mum," Nancy said freezing her face into a death-mask. "Though I wanted to smash the thing, I knew she'd paid good money for it and all the rest of it. But I was so sure I was getting a puppy…I'd even bought a collar and lead."

"Disappointment can be hard to deal with," ventured Percy wriggling on his seat as the bark bit into him.

Bringing her chin up and fixing him with her pretty blue-green eyes that had just a film of moisture over them, Nancy told him, "I was going to call him Panky."

Percy looked at her with compassion and thought how much he'd like to see her with a dog.

Chapter 4
Their First Adventure

Nancy awoke smiling and her smile broadened as the day ahead dawned on her. She continued to smile across the breakfast table at her mother, right up until she waved Fern off through the front door with a, "Have a good day at work, mum."

Then it was off with her uniform. She snatched goodies from around the kitchen and replaced her school work with them and proceeded down the garden path not stopping to admire the colourful clusters of newly planted pansies. She was on a mission, the zeal of which was symptomatic of the very young or neurologically diverse.

Percy also awoke from his nocturnal slumber with a frisson of excitement as he anticipated an extraordinary day. Trepidation met him at the bathroom mirror as he brushed his teeth with extra vigour.

The excitement was building and as he climbed into the family car it coursed through his veins and he wondered if his voice was just a little tense as he asked his dad to drop him off someway before the school.

"We're early Dad. Let me walk from here,"
"But your mum said only from Roseland Road,"
"Well Mrs Truffit said everyone else in my class is allowed to."

Mr Baskerville pulled the Volvo over. Percy scrambled out but not after giving the sleepy Ada's hair an affectionate rustle and his dad a heartfelt thank you. Then he stood on the pavement and watched his dad drive out of sight. *"It is happening,"* he told himself and felt a little peculiar. *"It is on."*

He hadn't felt this level of excitement since the time his Uncle Bob took him sledging on Edge Hill. He'd hurtled down steep obstacle-strewn snow, slicing through ice ridden slopes on a red plastic toboggan, out of control.

His mother had noticed the glow and glower of her young son as he'd limped up the stairs hanging onto the banisters "How was your Bob-sleighing," she'd laughed.

And here she was worried about him walking down Tulip Avenue by himself. He continued walking with his with head down and his heart-rate lifted.

From the opposite direction Nancy came walking along Hyacinth Avenue with her lips pursed, almost at a whistle. There they met at the corner as planned.

"Remember if anyone asks, it's a Teacher Training Day. Or you're Home-schooled."

It occurred to Percy that might wash for a new pupil but most folk knew what's what in the village.

"Chill them beans," she said as Percy's face revealed his worry.

"It's all about the risk…reward ratio," she told him.

She was so cool thought Percy. This was not the first time she'd bunked off, or indeed drawn along a male companion.

At her previous school it had only taken a packet of fun-size mars bars to persuade the young Edward to accompany her on her first donkey-based heist.

Percy had been altogether a harder nut to crack than Edward. She had had to give Percy the full works. Told him of the letter she'd sent to Father Christmas for a zebra. How she planned to call it Stripe and keep it in the garden shed and how **all** she'd got for her troubles was a stuffed Beanie. She'd fought a hard battle to manage her expectations.

Now she confessed to Percy, "There was this boy at my last school. Well, there was an incident with a donkey."
"Donkey gate," offered Percy lightening up but wishing they could get out of the village and into the relative safety of the countryside.
"Under a velvet blue sky, we spied him grazing. He was caramel and the most beautiful donkey that had ever lived. Two long straight ears and pleasing confirmation. Tall for a donkey, the healthiest and fittest of them all and an obvious born leader. In hindsight, he was the wrong choice all together but I was seven. What did I know?" she turned to Percy and lifted her hand and shoulders in a winning gesture.

Percy who didn't know much about donkeys said nothing.

"Beautiful but not gentle…" she continued.
"With a deep-rooted adversity to authority?" offered Percy thinking of his little sister.
"We managed to get him through the gate. I actually thought we'd get him home. This donkey did have the most perfect dark brown cross on its back. Its ears when forward were like two soldiers on duty. You know outside their sentry boxes…We didn't get very far. This car honked its horn and that was it. The donkey shot off…giving an alarm far louder than the car! No match for an eight-year-old boy. Top tip: don't wind the rope round your hand."
Nancy thought back to poor Edmund's body, face down, being dragged along for at least ten metres.
"The damage to his uniform took some explaining," she recounted thinking he probably still bore the scars. "To do Edmund justice…he was a very fast runner," she added.
"But no match for a burrow on the bolt?" said Percy.
"I can still hear the bray. Took to its freedom like a zebra in the Okavango, off on migration…tail in the air, wind in its face."

They turned off the road on to a footpath away from the village and Percy felt the relief.

As if he realized that he wasn't on the great Argentinian Bank Robbery but just turning out off Fishpond's Road for a walk in the country.

The path began to get a little muddy. Percy slipped a couple of times.

"You ought to get your parents to welly-up. How long have you lived here?"

Percy said nothing but carried on beside her.

"I'm yet to leave footprints in the mud," said Nancy by way of apology.

"I can see you doing something worthwhile Percy...even remarkable."

Percy fluttered within and wondered what it might be and the mud, even though it was becoming thicker, didn't seem so much of an encumbrance.

"Anyway, this donkey...was on the loose...every time we got close to him such as when he stopped to graze on the grass verge, he'd be off,

"A shooting star," said Percy picturing the scene.

"That's what we called him!" claimed Nancy. "But this time we have experience and better equipment." She jangled the halter in one hand and a bag of carrots in the other.

Meanwhile, back in the classroom, Miss McBride felt the absence of Nancy. The classroom seemed

flat without her. The girls' latest dance routine, in the absence of Nancy's acrobatic flare, lacked *va va voom*.
Miss McBride had been trying for a baby for three years. The doctor had said there was nothing wrong with her and to *keep trying*.

Keep trying! It was something she might say to a pupil when they missed the ball in a game of rounders.

This was the thirty-sixth consecutive month that she'd been met with disappointment. At thirty-six years old she felt adrift. *Was this it now?*

Noah Taylor wasn't the only one that morning to be struggling with new concepts.

Chapter 5
Fields of Green

Nancy and Percy began their long hike by clambouring over a style into their first open field. Nancy couldn't help but consider that this walk was just like life, a set of obstacles to get over, through or under and in so doing it was useful not to lose sight of their surrounding beauty.

By the time he was crossing the third field Percy was more than a little fed up of traipsing several metres behind. Nancy moved too quickly. He was forever having to keep up.

Even once off the seriously muddy path and on the firmer footings of grassland Percy found it challenging. He wasn't keeping up and the sight of her so far ahead was increasingly annoying.

It was the longest walk he'd ever done. And despite it being just ten-thirty. Percy was keen to start the picnic. In the excitement of that morning he'd only managed one Weetabix, instead of his usual two, and completely foregone the banana topping. He had hoped to double breakfast but

Nancy who had all their provisions just kept on walking.

"And you say *these* donkeys are near here?" he asked as they rested by the gate.

"Ah…by car," said Nancy shamelessly.

"Mum took me there as a bribe to avoid **The Dog Talk**. It isn't that far. I've got a map and a mobile."

"I'm not allowed a mobile on school days," said Percy who wasn't allowed a mobile for chunks of the weekend either.

"Your parents are so cool. Though, I could see your mum having you chipped," said Nancy.

Percy looked down at his trouser legs. They were covered with mud and there were clods of mud around his trainers.

At the next fence, Nancy did a gate flip. Percy dragged himself over it and they made their way across the field that followed. It was ploughed and proved hard going.

Indeed, Percy felt on the edge of good temper as he slithered and slipped for what seemed like an eternity. He was losing confidence in the whole affair. He knew Nancy desperately wanted a dog but to let her desires spill over to vitriolic remarks about his mother and at his expense was a bit rich.

Though he could imagine his mother with some sort of injecting device slapping it into his thigh *for his own benefit*. After all you never did know who the next ransom victim might be for a random fanatical freedom fighter hiding behind the village post box. Percy wondered his worth. That was the key to life. Well one of the keys on a whole bunch of them. *Know your worth.*

Of course, you might think you know your worth and others might not agree, he pondered, confusing himself. Of something he was sure as Nancy marched further into the distance. She knew hers.

He ploughed on. It was eleven. They'd be having break at school and biscuits and here he was in the midst of thick sludge and he didn't really like donkeys. It wasn't that he had anything against them. He'd hardly ever thought of them until this venture.

It wouldn't be so bad if the field they were in wasn't ploughed. He'd thought the last section of the footpath bad enough but in comparison to this it had been a joy. Now moving forward was hard.

Step by step you had to pull yourself out of the mire.

He wondered what it was like to be a soldier. How did they manage? And those camp followers probably not so well kitted?

A loud scream broke his train of miserable thoughts. It was Nancy. She'd turned to him, arms in the air and was twirling and whooping in some sort of exposition.

At least it gave him a chance to catch up. He squelched through the mud towards her. By the time he'd got to her she had stopped her whirling and was as calm as a newsreader.

It struck him that although he'd lived in Langton Green for many years, he'd never heard of this field of donkeys.

Nancy sounded like a straight talker but could she be guilty of gross exaggeration? Disingenuous… and a wee bit ruthless, maybe.

She had recovered from her *dervish* and they were now side by side with Nancy taking the worst side

right in the plough. The next field was in sight.
"Percy," she said as if addressing a knight.
"Yes?"
"Faint heart never won Fair Donkey," she said and pushed him.

Percy failed to remove his look of underwhelment.
"Exercise good Percy. Two legs better. You look as if you *is* on The Long March," she laughed and marched off in front of him as if once he was out of sight he would be out of mind and she could fully focus on her destination.
"Have you ever seen these donkeys?" he called after her.
"Seen one! I sponsor one," she shouted back but didn't stop.
"Minky," she shouted and picked up the pace.

It was lucky the next field now in view was green because if it had been brown Percy would have given up. He'd have risked a bullet in the back to free himself from the annoyingness of the situation. Why was Nancy so whole-hearted about this? It wasn't even her number one aim. Everyone who spent five minutes with Nancy knew she wanted a dog. He could only assume that Minky was some sort of rescue animal and wasn't certain if Nancy had ever been to this donkey place in person.

He picked up the pace too and again they found themselves by a five-barred gate. But this time Nancy was holding it open for him and she looked quite contrite but then spoiled it by quoting, "We are all in paradise but refuse to see it."
Percy didn't give her the satisfaction of asking who'd said it.

"I went with Mum once …but all the donkeys were in the yard for this open day. So, yes, I have been to the place but haven't the exact blue print," she clarified.

Percy welcomed the honesty. It would have been gym at school and it was his least favourite lesson. Brown upon brown of ploughed grooves stretched right up to the hedge line on either side.

"Parallel lines," he said as enigmatically as someone with vastly inappropriate footwear could in the same situation. He skirted round Nancy and the gate and put his back to the plough and moved off with renewed vigour putting aside the toughness of human existence. Sink your foot right down in to it and haul it out.

"Got a little dirt on my boots," sang Nancy soon catching him up.
"Hey…my dad has that one," said Percy.
"Nutin like an open road," drawled Nancy as if a character in a William Faulkner novel.
"Got a little dirt on my boots," Percy laughed but felt even Scott and Shackleton stopped for a game of cards every now and then.

On they walked and Percy couldn't help thinking how much less labour intensive it was to be a sea voyager. His innate fear of sharks extended to all things murky underwater.

His mind was drifting as he remembered how on his stay at uncle's this phobia was born. On a visit to London he and Uncle Bob were just settling into the film *Jaws* when there was an urgent knocking at the door. In burst a heavily pregnant woman and her suitably nervous partner. They had urgent use of the birthing pool which had been installed in Bob's study with his complete permission on account of it being on the ground floor and up to weight.

He'd never forget baby Heath born that night in the apartment in Hampstead. It was all very exciting but they'd had Jaws playing all the way through and it had left quite an impression.

Percy mused that when a person was trampling through the countryside, one foot in front of the other, the mind had plenty of time to roam. *At least he wasn't carrying the kit.* At the very start he had offered but Nancy had said *Na* and he wasn't going to ask again.

They'd stopped talking some time back and broken back into single file. Nancy stopped briefly on occasions and just nosed the air…bit like his Uncle's Welsh Springer Spaniel. It was not the first time she'd reminded him of the beloved Gwendoline. It wasn't so much the colouring but the energy. *And the sense of purpose.*

Nancy stood still and waited for him to catch up. "And now," she said with a measure of magnanimity. "A fifteen-minute lunch break." Percy collapsed on a plastic shopping bag he had the foresight to secrete into a trouser pocket before departure.

Nancy tore off her backpack and spreading out her jacket, declared. "Grubs up," and he sidled up beside her.

The girl pulled the goodies from the bag and held them up one by one for inspection.
"Cheese straws," she said dropping them on the shared space directly in front of them protected from the ground by a black woollen scarf.
"Crisps!" Percy said with his spirits beginning to soar. "And white bread," he stared at Nancy and back to the baguette that had been twisted back on itself to fit in the backpack. He gasped as if in heaven.
"Peanut butter and jam," said Nancy gayly as she dropped the jars into the mix.
"Ohhhh! All my favourites Nance. All my favourites," said Percy, all earthly ills evaporating for that moment.
"Goodness," Nancy said as she pulled out a chocolate bar, "you're morphing into a yellow Labrador Perc. And dogs are allergic to *chocolat,*" assuming a French accent and pretending for a split second to put the chocolate back in the bag. Percy was watching the chocolate as it made its way in and back out of the bag…but had

considered he was going to eat his crisps and baguette first and then the cheese straw and then **chocolate**.

"Do you need a spittoon!" finalized Nancy pulling out two generously sized smoothies. "Berry…or banana. Too late. You get Berry," and she dropped the smoothie into his lap. "Look around you Percy. This is the best playground in the world."

"Would have picked Berry anyway," he said as he opened the bag of sea salted Crisps thinking how his mother would have never allowed any of this into the house. "If it comes claiming that it's good for your health, it will mean it's bad for you…take sweeteners…," he could hear his mother's voice. There they feasted on that late February school day, far from the madding crowd of maths and PE lessons, far from their respective households. They sat, oblivious to the outside world of towns, of villages, of cars and people, just the three of them, Nancy, Percy and Nature. Free as can be, and in the broad sense time still very much on their side.

Nancy was quite pleased the bag was lighter but kept it to herself as she gradually realised she had got her timing, in the immediate sense, quite badly out. She remembered Christopher Columbus' double charts, his flagrant lies to the crew, his absurd reckoning that Cuba was Japan or Hispania, China. He'd made the inhabitants on pain of death swear that they weren't on an island even though they all knew they were.

No, she didn't have it in her to keep Percy in the dark. She would have to tell him that she didn't quite know where the field of donkeys was and it had taken them a lot longer to get to this point than she had anticipated. They would have to leave in the next half an hour if they had a hope of getting back on time.

She resolved to tell him, but not yet. They were **so** nearly there. Go big or go home. They had to be very close. They'd been on the trail since nine and it was now past twelve. Why did February have to get dark by five and why was she so worried on Percy's behalf that he would get into trouble?

They would travel off the footpath and take the next field diagonally. Nancy sniffed the air and thought she could detect a faint equine whiff.

Torn between her desire to set foot in a world of donkeys and run her fingers through Minky's fur and a duty of care towards Percy coupled with a minor fear of getting in trouble. Nancy found herself dithering by the next gate. *Should she stay now or should she go now?*

"As the crow flies," she instructed with a finger pointing diagonally to the midpoint of the next hedge-line.

"Stealth, remember stealth Percy," Nancy warned though she didn't think it was going to be a problem. No one could call Percy a loudmouth. "Bring out your inner cat," she smiled through her greenish-blue eyes. Percy clawed the air in a cat-claw, a half-hearted gesture. The joy of the picnic had worn off and he was aware of the time and he wasn't sure if he wasn't going to ditch her and turn home. He was almost certain of the route.

Maybe he should just try to stop her now and say something. The whole thing was so utterly out of his experience. A growing sense of worry was invading him. What would happen if his mother came back early and discovered him missing. The only thing in their favour was that it was slightly down hill on the way back. He thought of all the fields they'd come through and swallowed.

"Yes, Perc out of the shadows…bon! On y va!" Nancy declared as they made their way through yet another gate of discovery. The previous fields had been slightly up hill and the pair had slowly but surely ascended all morning.

A burst of excitement gripped Nancy. The field that followed was small. On the far side a thick hedge of hawthorn, not yet in bloom, shielded their vision. With renewed vigour they reached it in no time and scrambled through, taking little notice of a scratch here, a rip there, so wrapped up in a sense of urgency.

Nancy threw Percy a smile as if he'd helped her crack a safe full of treasure.
"We're going to do it," she said with triumph.
Percy felt out of his comfort zone.
"One last field" said Nancy shaking her head.
"Which way shall we take it? You wait til you see Minky! Fur like eiderdown. Loves a tickle under the chin."
Percy began to relax ...giving himself over to the final push. They walked towards a gap in this final straggly hedge-line.

From this plateau, out it spread: a deep valley of donkeys.

"Minky, Mokey, Gaia, Bathsheba, Zenobia, Bob," cried Nancy pulling out her binoculars she surveyed with the solemnity of an expert before handing them to Percy and taking some photos on her mobile. There they stood together, proud and silent. They had the vantage. The donkeys were little figures in the valley. Maybe fifteen or twenty …a herd.

Percy thought it might be the second or third most significant view of his life. There was a glory to it. He turned to Nancy.
"A rainbow of buffs, tans, browns, toffees and silvers," her mouth murmured, her eyes now round and face alight. "Haven't we done well Perc," she said sending a woolly feeling through him.

Time stood.
But then with no warning the wind picked up. The mute pair stood motionless as soft rain fell.
Silence remained as they looked down making calculations.
"They'll probably move to the barn. Their coats aren't waterproof," said Nancy.
The route down to them looked steep and Percy was almost certain that unless they turned back

soon they wouldn't make it home in time. He'd have to sort out his muddy clothes for one thing.

Then the hard rain fell and the words just tumbled out of him, "I want to go home."
"Percy, try not to over-expose," Nancy said still gawping at the donkeys. "Embrace impermanence."

Thunder cracked. Nancy stuffed her phone away. "Just because life's easier when the sun's out doesn't mean it's better. Don't be such a snowflake, Perc," she said. "It's just one foot after the other... I never got the chance to halter Minky," she declared holding Percy's arm.

"Dancing in the rain," muttered Percy and took his arm back.

Rain poured down her hatless head winding down her ringlets in streams before dripping off. "My Uncle Chris says, always leave a bite in the cherry," said Percy looking at her face.

Nancy hoped his uncle Chris never choked on the stone. She turned her back on the field of donkeys feeling like Livingstone at the rapids turning back after so much planning and so much effort.

"Oh! Brave New World that has such donkeys in it," shouted Nancy to the elements.

"Bottom would have been proud to be a part of such a glorious herd," said Percy beginning to feel very wet.

"You're a genius Perc," said Nancy tugging down her trousers and spinning her backside to the valley.

Now whose over-exposing thought Percy.

"Bottoms Up," urged Nancy "There's no policeman in the sky."

Lightening struck. The two children, silhouetted on the peak, burst out laughing.

"We live in the flicker," quoted Nancy. *"There is no denying the wild horse in us."*

Chapter 6
Great Expectations

Tuesday of half-term, Percy knocked on Nancy's front door. He was wearing a checked shirt with corduroy trousers and Nancy thought he cut quite a dash. She wondered if it was his parents doing. There had been absolutely no repercussions connected to *their Day Out*. Though Nancy only had to sing, "Got a little dirt on my boots," to spread a broad grin over Percy's face.

This was a welcome relief for Nancy as with the last donkey heist it had been a different story. A fact she had omitted to declare to Percy.

She recalled her mother standing across the doorway of their last house with her hands on her hips… always a sign of trouble.
Nancy had retaliated asking her mother if it was a crime to be born with great expectations and bolstering her defence with the age old *I never asked to be born* to which Nancy's mother retorted *and I never asked to have you* and slammed the door shut.

But it was nothing to the next day when Nancy

was called to see the head…and had to endure the ludicrous sight of the most full-of-herself woman, luxuriating in her swivel chair.
"Risible, shameless exploitation… such an unhealthy power imbalance. I had a damn good go in that chair before I left," she told Percy. "Miss Frobisher…she had me standing up defenceless, the other side of that wide desk as she spun in her chair attempting to end the circumference with a stern look."
Percy could picture it. Nancy could tell a story.
"I was determined to de-escalate it so put on this contrite act. Of course, I didn't mention Edmund so he got off scot free. My punishment was not being allowed to go on the school trip to Warwick Castle. I'd been very much looking forward to that trip. Mum who is nothing if not inconsistent took me anyway. We were moving so what better than to rock up at the castle and munch pies in front of Miss Frobisher. The old trout."

Percy couldn't imagine his parents in a thousand years doing anything like that.
"Anyway, enough of that. What have we got here?" she said with glee and whisked him through the yellow walled kitchen past the biscuit tin and into the centre of the garden where earlier

she'd prepared a makeshift work area.

Percy unclutched the impressively large oblong box labelled Young Chemist. Nancy jumped up and down.
"I wish I had a godmother, it's not even your birthday."
"Well she's my aunt, too. Aunt Lucy," qualified Percy.
"It must be the biggest one they make," said Nancy and took it from Percy.

She ripped open the box ...handing him the instruction booklet.
"Let the experiments begin!" she chuckled rubbing her hands with gleeful eyes twinkling so brightly that Percy wondered, and not for the first time, if Nancy had hailed from some other planet.
"It would be hilarious..." started Nancy and then collapsed into hearty laughter, unable to finish her sentence.
"Can you imagine... Mrs Truffit ...she'd have to..." Nancy started again through fits of giggles, quite irrepressible... "to come out of her office."
Again, they had to both wait for Nancy to gain composure. Seconds passed. "During school

time!" she finished collapsing in mirth. And repeated the punch line.

"She'd have to COME out of her office in school time!"

"Holding her nose," said Percy, in gentle mirth, mouth closed, eyes on Nancy letting the humour out through his nostrils in short bursts.

Nancy still standing threw her head back and with a hand pinching her nose marched round the table before collapsing on to her seat, legs cycling in the air. She let forth a series of snorts the like of which reminded Percy of a piglet rootling for grain in mud. Nancy completed this episode with a row of her own snuffles…an affectation cultivated to perfection through watching Peppa Pig. Then something caught her eye.

She fell upon the set, picking out phial after phial and opening packets of substance only to pick up her phone and follow some instruction. But Percy couldn't twig with any degree of certainty what she was concocting but had recently seen the film Oppenheimer and had read a worrisome account of Nobel and dynamite so when she held up a test tube and yelped, "Itching powder! Praise be to the Lord," he felt unnerved.

Though not brought up to any one particular faith Percy was uncomfortable about undermining any religious belief and against the indiscriminate spreading of anything bar maybe goodwill and smiles.

"I point blank refuse to be party to Itching Powder and so does my Chemistry set," he stated.

Nancy took a long look at him and respected his stance…for that afternoon anyway. *For goodness sake Its not Sargon gas* she felt like protesting but didn't.

"Stink bomb it is then," she decreed.

The whole surface area of Percy's wide mouth broke into a smile.

"Why Perc you are the energy that makes things happen," she said gesturing to the open box, then clapping her hands silently.

"Let it rip," said Percy with the fake action of stirring a pot.

And so they carried on under the pale grey sky. The young pair worked, mixing and matching and sniffing and pouring and having an immensely fun time. It was only blighted slightly by Nancy's suggestion that they drag out the camping stove from the shed to *cook* something up. Percy just wasn't ready for it.

"Well wouldn't it be brill if we not only stunk Mrs Truffit's office out, but got her when she had one of those bigwig inspectors in?"

Percy didn't think they were due an inspection as the school had just recently been awarded Outstanding.

"I think a Governor would constitute fair game…give them something to amuse dinner guests with," said Percy.

Nancy couldn't think of Fern ever having dinner guests.

"Biscuit break, Percy," she suggested.

"Pleeese…You are soo, soo lucky. I'm never alone at my house and I have a very naughty little sister."

"Ah the balance of blessings," said Nancy who'd have given anything for a sister.

Percy who didn't actually have any axe to grind and actively liked Mrs Truffit, hoped the effect of the stink bomb would be minor. Nancy agreed with him that actually the teachers at Langton were, in general, very nice. They decided to carry out their deed on a Friday because it was Miss

McBride's day off and Year 5 was stuck with the rather unprepossessing Miss Palfrey.

The chief defect of Miss Palfrey in Nancy's view was that she always asking Nancy for the answers even if her hand wasn't up.
"It's true I know the answers but *Spread the joy*, I told her the other day, rather abruptly. The class burst out laughing. I felt terrible but would she *hide the papayas.*"
Percy hadn't heard the phrase but got the idea.
"No," continued Nancy "just went on asking. So, then I started asking her, "What was the Papal stance on Lutherism? Did the blood swollen leeches from Henry's vile ulcerated leg crawl on to any of his Mrs's before he had their heads hacked off with an axe? Well since then she's given me a wider berth but I think she's said something to that French teacher."
"Ah Miss Howard, with the black horn-rimmed glasses taped up with cellotape. I hate it when she stalks around the class room and then suddenly picks someone to read?" said Percy.
"Yes, that one. She's all strange with me now," said Nancy.
"Probs cos you can actually speak French," said Percy.

"Suspect she's never set foot in any French speaking nation. Did you know mum and I used live in Normandy on account of her romance with Pierre? We went for a holiday and just sort of …stayed on. He worked there. It was a great summer. Lots of kids… and not tied to their parents, either. Swimming every day. Mum was so relaxed and happy. Had my fifth birthday there. Pierre organized this amazing cake. It arrived with five sparkling candles and sculptured pink frosting with hundreds and thousands and *Nancy* in thin, white italics written across it."

"What happened?" asked Percy.

"Pierre was very sweet. Did his best to keep Mum happy but she got homesick so after a cosy winter spent in town above a Boulangerie and a final summer of love at the campsite we came back. But it did mean I had a whole year at a French School," explained Nancy.

"And you got to live above a Boo-longe- er-rie," said Percy.

"Vraiment," said Nancy and lapped her pink tongue around her lips.

"I bet Year 5 was impressed that you can speak French?" he said.

"Well I didn't overdo it. I could understand every word **she** said but Mrs Howard struggled to understand me. Something about the dialect, **she** said. "Too colloquial."

"Rude," said Percy.

"Asked her whether it was true that the Ballerinas depicted with such grace by the likes of Degas were nicknamed *Les Petites Rats* by the Great and the Good ….and why?" said Nancy.

Percy wasn't sure what she meant by that.

That quiet Friday afternoon Nancy delivered the bomb. No cameras enabled her to drop it practically in plain sight. One couldn't fault her operative skills. Assigned to a minor clerical task which put her in the vicinity the opportunity struck when Mrs Truffit's door opened and she strolled over to have a word with Mrs Fudge, on reception.

In a blink of an eye, Nancy slid into the empty office and dropped off the package. In and out in a flash.

"No disturbances please Mrs Fudge I've got the Planning Application to get through," Mrs Truffit said firmly striding back to her office and shutting the door.

"Rather you than me," called out the incredibly good-natured Mrs Fudge.

No one could have detected the surge of power that had ripped through Nancy's young body as she'd placed the item in the waste paper bin under Mrs Truffit's desk. Emerging from the safety of the loos Nancy walked back to class with her chest pounding but with a face of innocence and an unbreakable smile.

"Thank you **so** much," said Miss Palfrey to Nancy as she slipped back into class and then slid into her desk.

Minutes later the school was in chaos.

The launch of the stink bomb went well but its outcome didn't. The smell was vile. Windows were opened and there was a marked degree of fuss especially from Year 3 whose classroom was the nearest to the repugnant odour. Ella and Logan, the Baker twins couldn't stop retching and had to be taken to the playground where they threw up, dramatically.

This interfered with Year 6's games lesson and in consequence Miss Trott made a very poor referee decision which led to some ugly name-calling. In temper she cancelled all away matches for that term. Parents that evening were to manage all sorts of disappointment. It really wasn't fair.

After the bomb, just about every member of staff was on the back foot including the usually stalwart Mr Dockery who wouldn't come out of his shed due to the Baker twins vomiting. Ella threw up all over his petunias and Maya all over the netball post. The playground stank nearly as bad as the school.

An emergency whole school assembly had soon followed where Nancy and Percy shot glances at each across the hall. Percy dropped his eyes to the floor as not to invite detection before the whole school had to file out into the school playground. Had not Mrs Truffit the longstanding arrangement of a bridge game at her house that evening at six she might have been persuaded by the much more risk adverse Mrs Fudge, the school secretary, to call services.

"Which?" Mrs Truffit had asked.

"All of them," Mrs Fudge suggested.

"Nonsense. We'll practice for the concert. Get Miss Trombone to take over."

"Miss Tucker?" said Mrs Fudge not sure if Miss Tucker was up to it at such short notice.

"Yes, that one. She can do a singing lesson with them when we sort out this mess," said Mrs

Truffit. "It'll aerate the lungs." And she winked at Mrs Fudge.

The smell became worse not better. It was more potent than Nancy bargained for and she had to prevent herself from catastrophising. *If I get caught my chances of getting a dog…*

Mrs Truffit's peach silk shirt was on display having removed her jacket. She was striding around the playground in faultless attire like a military commander. She asked if anyone had something to sing whilst Miss Tucker composed herself and took over.

Nancy stepped forward and without a trace of embarrassment or hint of fuss or whatsoever any musical accompaniment sang the Dido song like a bird. The staff, the whole of Year Six and most of Year Five were transported. Percy noticed his teacher Miss Clements wipe a tear. The smallest children fiddled a bit but she was an out and out success uplifting the school to a better humour.

Nancy was normally not one for singing to an audience, although sang all the time at home. But on this occasion, the school facing such adversity, felt it the very least she could do.

Unfortunately, it didn't stop Mrs Truffit drilling down with her inquiry. A few remarks were made about the personal hygiene in Year 6. Then there followed laughter and a great deal of whispering.

"If anyone knows a single thing about this, they must come forward," said Mrs Truffit.
Absolute silence followed but there was a lot of looking around, including Nancy and Percy. *Ha if that's goin to happen.*

Mrs Fudge and most of the teachers embarked on calling parents for an early pick up. Mrs Tucker hampered by the absence of a piano or any musical accompaniment failed to get the school singing so Year Six were allowed home. With the exception of Percy, who still hadn't persuaded his mother to retract her stance. In the meantime, Nancy's mother had asked that Nancy should be allowed to do the walk home so Nancy was free to go. She gave Percy the teeniest of waves as she left through the gate.

It was tempting to tell her mother. Fern was so much in two camps that her legs had to encompass quite a divide. Though anti-establishment at heart she'd gone to some lengths to find this Outstanding School in the leafy village of Langton Green to advance her daughter's prospects in this tough old world.

Chapter 7
Double Figures

Concerning the stink-bomb, there had been no comeback. Miss McBride **had** given Nancy a quizzing look that Monday morning and murmured 1666. This was met with a deadpan smile.

Nancy felt they were out of the woods but never-the-less had woken that morning with a heightened sense of unease and this feeling seemed to be gaining traction.

She shrugged her shoulders and suspected it was about her forthcoming birthday. She didn't like the prospect of double figures. Her stomach seemed out of kilter and she forced her shoulders down and insisted that she would walk to school that day despite a bag full of books.
"But it's on my way," said Fern.

At times like these you have to top up the treats she told Percy as they rubbed shoulders at the corner of Fishpond's as nonchalantly as two firm friends can.

Nancy tried to extract a promise that they would do some out of school heist before Nancy hit ten.
"I need to commit to something…before Mens Rea culpability thing bangs in," she said seriously.
"Yes, but…" said Percy.
"It needn't be for financial gain… maybe for rights. Yes, Animal Rights. We could free minks!" said Nancy.
"Yes, but…" said Percy.
Percy wondered if she'd ever consider unintended consequences.
"Could go Green, I suppose. The planet is frying and dying," said Nancy.
"But I'm eleven. I'd be accountable. What **is** the legal situation with minors?" said Percy.
Nancy stopped.
"Well I could have a cocktail party instead?" said Nancy determined to mark her tenth.

There was silence but Percy could almost hear the squeezing of many neurons and synapses as a brain already on fire was racked.
"With panache," she added. "You could invite three or four of your class just to give it an edge you know how it goes… none of the drips …maybe Devak, Alexander, Aiden, and Jamilla.

Who's that girl with the very long hair that has a cousin with the Irish Wolf Hound."

"Ella Harman," said Percy in a thin voice wondering if he'd ever actually spoken to her. He didn't think he had.

"A party is a good idea," he agreed and didn't correct her use of the word Cocktail instead of Mocktail, or that she was asking of him far too much.

"A party it is," beamed Nancy. "It would be a good way of coming out, Perc…you and me. We could hang out more at school."

"Maybe think of a theme Nancy," suggested Percy.

"Fairytales," Nancy exploded "Sounds childish but it can be ohh soooo wild…it could go anywhere…I can taste the freedom of united self-expression. It's going to be so mega amazing," said Nancy "And you are not going to see my outfit until the day of the party," she announced as they split to enter the school separately.

For a short while Nancy's urge to get a dog lessened as she concentrated on the party. Shifting her reward systems involved feasting her eyes on material and sourcing sumptuous brocade, and losing herself in imaginings of herself in a huge crinoline, stepping into a glass carriage pulled by six white horses or at the very least amidst six white mice and a generously sized pumpkin.

Fern was delighted with the idea of a party. The two discussed games, prizes, food layout even music and agreed the notion that one had to ask the whole class was nonsense.
"It's not that you know all of them and besides there's a recession. Quality over quantity in a case like this," said Fern.
"Quality of quantity, in't it?" said Nancy.
"Double figures need a proper celebration." Fern agreed and they both shook their heads.

Fern rather spoilt this moment of family bliss by insisting on a fist bump. Nancy hoped she would keep herself scarce during the party and wondered if she could be induced to go out at least for part of it.

They discussed dips and were keen to make sure the vegetarians were well catered for but decided the vegans could bring their own.
"Besides," said Fern "Essentially it's a drinks and dress-up affair."

Over the course of the weekend Nancy designed invitations with the intention to hand them out the following Monday. She jotted a to-do list and made a mental timeframe of getting them done. Fern laboured with some very heavy duty burnt orange velvet curtains to create a s*tunning* dress for Cinderella. But by Sunday morning Nancy was having grave doubts of her ability to source white mice.

"I'm to be in bottle green silk and blood red," she told Fern. "I'm not Cinders anymore but the Wicked Queen."

Nancy's face was so triangular, her poise so perfect, her gaze so shafting, for a split second her own mother felt quite unsettled. Fern put down the scissors and followed Nancy to her bedroom and with a head round the doorway said, "Very regal bearing…our family…I'm pretty sure we're a direct line from the Queen of Sweden via a French route. Your great, great, great etc was engaged to the young Napoleon…threw him over and married Royalty. History doesn't relate why though I do know that it's on record that Napoleon had scabies."

Nancy wasn't sure how much to believe when Fern made these grandiose remarks but wasn't uncomfortable with the connection.
"Blue blood like the Nautilus family," Nancy said throwing herself on her bed. "But not three hearts," she said. "Yes, Mum. The class Cephalopoda… Cuttlefish, Squids and the Octopi have blue blood and three hearts."
"A useful blessing," said Fern.
"Undoubtedly," said Nancy giving Fern a loving get-out-of-my-bedroom look.

Lying on her bed one leg crossed over the other, Nancy had wondered why she hadn't gone for the Pirate theme that Perc had proffered. At the time, she had been completely ignorant of what's her name, that pirate in charge of some forty thousand, who had terrified everyone in the South China Seas. She had been without mercy.

On Sunday afternoon when Percy came around, an agitated Nancy was not her normal self.
"Did the Wright brothers give up with their first draw back…no it was try, try and fly again… all Orvil and his bro had was a shed and their dreams. Bit of bird study, aerodynamic stuff the propelling stuff was almost secondary and there

they were up in the sky. All I need is some wheels…and six white horses," she lamented. "Can't even get mice. I'm not sure about the party. You haven't told anyone have you?" she asked. He hadn't.

The truth of the matter was Nancy had just found out that Abigail, too, had birthday plans for that day and had got her invites out already.

Nancy couldn't reconceptulize and declared to her mother and Percy she was done with the idea. "But you were so keen?" he said appearing neither disappointed or surprised. He hadn't been averse to dressing up as a wolf but had begun to worry about getting the costume sourced. His parents weren't that type. He said he had to go home because they had people round. Fern cleared away her curtains.

That evening Nancy still determined to mark her double figures in some way, had reverted to notions of lawlessness and was keen to take advantage of still being nine.
"We strictly wouldn't hurt anybody, *not cat nor canary*. We'll use stealth," she told Percy when they walked home from school on Monday.

"Cat burglary?" Percy replied not known for his dexterity on the ropes at the school gym.
He was a natural law-abider and found the whole concept uncomfortable.
"Maybe a shoplifting jaunt!" Nancy suggested brightly.
Percy was glad that she seemed to be in good spirits as she'd appeared a little flat after the Mocktail fancy dress party idea had been scrapped. Fern had taken him to one side before he'd left the house and asked him what he thought might cheer her up. "A puppy," he'd said and Fern's face had dropped and she'd gone back upstairs.
"When mum worked at Home Bargain's I saw loads of it," said Nancy. "Even with that big cardboard cut-out of a police man. The art is to wear the right clothing."
"Big pockets," offered Percy.
It was clear to Nancy that Percy had no aptitude for petty crime and life hadn't been hard enough to corrupt the little fellow. It soured any pleasure at the thought of taking a *whip round* as she wouldn't want him to get into trouble. She had thoughts of doing a *loop-scoop* alone but it held no real attraction.
"Think bigger,"

"What we need is to go on an adventure to Australia. I have an aunt there," she said though she had no such thing.

"Oh, I would **so** love to see a Dingo," she said and beamed at Percy with such brightness he couldn't help by being caught up in the attraction.

"The whole wildlife is amazing," he agreed.

"And it has rain forest," yelped Nancy who now was jumping up and down.

"You're a genius. Percy a genius. We can always rely on you to come up with the corkers!"

Now Percy was beaming. He'd had an ample amount of *well-dones* from his parents, especially his father who seemed to give him a well done for anything but he couldn't remember being so swelled with pride as Nancy made him. It was like standing in front of a mirror and seeing yourself magnified.

They decided to return to Nancy's after school, as Percy was keen to take full advantage of having some time to himself. Mondays and Wednesdays were when his vociferous little sister Ada stayed late at the childminders.

Chapter 8
Assault

In the end, for her birthday, Fern took Nancy to London. They did London Zoo and the Dungeons and a river trip all in one day. They had lunch in a pub near Regent's Park. Nancy was restored to good humour.

She greeted Percy the next day as if she'd been to Paris not London. She air-kissed his cheeks three times in the continental fashion.
"Come on in, Old Bean," said the smiling Nancy, "I was licked by an Okapi at the zoo. It had a long blue tongue."

With swift actions she served up a juice carton and sat down opposite Percy. An orientally decorated biscuit tin, newly bought in London, had been placed in a central position.
"Did you know they hid Crown jewels in a Biscuit tin during the Blitz? Shame you're not more suitably attired," she commented.

He removed his hand from the biscuit tin with a milk digestive attached to it and hoped there would be no hike involved.

"Just out back," Nancy explained now gesturing for him to follow her out into the garden.

It did bemuse Percy this ability of hers, to sometimes read his thoughts.

"We could do an assault course," said Nancy who had clearly worked everything out as she pulled various items from the garden shed.

Percy looked on dubiously despite Nancy's effort to fully involve him.

"Over here Perc…" she'd call waving and pointing. "Over there, Perc…no, not the green one. We're more equine than military," she explained with her hands on her hips, indicating a mass of bamboo sticks perched on various items to make a series of jumps.

"Shall we walk the course?" she said with an enthusiasm Percy did not yet feel and wasn't convinced that he ever would.

"So, the first's over the plastic watering cans, then you have that line of suitcases. Three's the jump made out of flower pots and well you can work it out. We don't need to number them as it's just us," said Nancy pointing out the sharp bend to the ultimate fence.

"Nancy, you're a very physical individual," Percy said.

"Think I will make numbers next time so we can alter the course," decided Nancy.

"I'm reserving judgement," said Percy who was pretty sure even at this stage of the game it wasn't going to be his favourite way of spending his free time. Although he had to admit building the course had been fun.

After a brief rest to admire their handiwork Nancy bounced out of her chair and started to canter round the garden. "I'm Whiskey," she told him adding, as she cantered past him, "I'm a 13.2hh Welsh Mountain crossed Connemara". Percy didn't know what that was but ascertained it was something fancy, with spirit. Whiskey performed an impeccable clear round.

Percy fell into the role of announcer and also suggested he timed the rounds. Nancy thought that was an excellent idea. After Whiskey came Blaze-away and then Go-Go. Then Tempo, Cromwell, Candy, Dinky, Dandy… the list went on and on. As well as commentating Percy timed the rounds and kept a note. He had a natural leaning for his newly-found position. "And now we have Go-go, a five- year-old chestnut fresh from Warwickshire competing for the first time in the Nancy Renard Stakes." He'd then clap, do a jeer or two and follow up with something like, "Could this be a clear round?"

This in turn was followed by a lot of clicking sounds from Nancy who seemed to be simultaneously horse and rider and very prone to geeing-up. Nancy, before she cantered through the two green-ribboned bamboo canes that marked the start, displayed some impressive spiraling.

Unfortunately, she didn't content herself with all this and approached Percy with an unwelcomed suggestion.

"Come on now Percy. You get hold of my T-Shirt and we'll go around together," she said pawing the ground with her foot.

Percy was reluctant. Nancy insisted.

"It'll be fine," she assured him and whinnied forcefully.

Whipped up with the excitement of it she turned her back to him.

"Jump on."

The two of them started up the garden but were sorely out of step. For one thing, Nancy was cantering and Percy running. Hardly seeing where he was going, it was all it he could do to stop himself tripping up.

He let go before the first fence and plonked himself back on the canvas chair with his legs out in protest, glad that he'd drawn the line. It was nearly the cause of a row but Nancy just tore passed him flicking her heels out in a mock buck and gave a particularly shrill whiney as if to say it all.

Without much discussion and with Percy still cooling off Nancy changed the course. "It's dog-agility now," she said after having added a series of large compost bags to crawl through and a bending lane out of bamboo sticks. After studying Percy's expression, she lowered all the fences considerably.

Percy by this stage had got off his chair and was helping with the poles. As Nancy measured them conscientiously with her feet he'd ram them into the ground.
"Teamwork," she said smiling.
Percy grinned back, and in a further effort to reconciliate, agreed to trial the new course.
"I'm a Spanish Water dog," he said.

Nancy clapped her hands together in delight. She cheered him on even though she felt his round was very slow.

Nancy, then had several goes. First as a Beagle, then a German Shepherd and then a Lurcher. Percy thought she hadn't really differentiated sufficiently but didn't say anything. She was working up to bringing out her inner Border collie.

Then Nancy, again going too far in Percy's opinion, wanted to double up. He was to be the dog and she, the owner, and they would do the round together.
"I'd rather be the owner," he'd said.
"Fine," she'd said and sprinted round on all fours spectacularly.
Two legs better than four he thought but said nothing.
Nancy then said she wanted her turn. Well, he wasn't keen but didn't refuse.
"Percy, are you a ruiner?" she asked.

Capitulating, he dropped onto all-fours but was so slow that less than a quarter way round and well before the garden waste obstacle, Nancy threw in the towel muttering something about him being absolutely hopeless.

It quite took the shine off the afternoon and Nancy could barely look at him. Nancy had declined his offer to clear up the course. Rather downcast he gathered his belongings. She was noisily putting things away when she caught sight of him opening the back gate. She came of the shed still carrying the red watering can and called after him, "Don't you want some toast?"

It was their normal habit to feast after an activity. Percy could never resist marmite. Or Peanut butter and jam. Or honey. And Nancy had all of them. He wasn't allowed bleached bread at home and even though Fern had taken to getting fifty/fifty, it was still an absolute treat. They sat back out in the garden and chewed through a pyramid of toast triangles.

Nancy never one to shy away from passing on nuggets of gleaned knowledge said, "Exercise breaks up your muscles and you need protein to build them up. Fat and carbohydrates give the body fuel but protein mends and improves it…so I am informed."

"Do you want the last triangle of protein?" asked Percy

"No Perc I would very much like you to have it," she said and smiled.

"I wish we were old enough to go on that *Race across the World* programme. I'd like to take mum abroad," said Nancy.

"Well maybe one day…"

"No Perc I'd like to go in the summer holidays. Would your parents let you go?"

"Probably," though he wasn't sure. "His mum might be glad of a rest but then again it would depend if it was deemed educational. He thought his dad might miss him and was pretty sure both parents would miss his input with his naughty little sister."

"Mmm, should think they'd be nervous," Nancy noted. "We need money," she went on. "I suppose we get it by robbing, gambling, sponsorship. Let's be sensible and take the middle option. Besides, even if we can't go away on some far-flung adventure I need money for Doggy Day care."

"Gambling. Shouldn't think it's that easy," said Percy choosing not to point out to Nancy that she didn't have a dog.

"House always wins does it, Percy?" said Nancy.

"Think so," said Percy who knew very little on the subject.

"Well, all we need do is infiltrate, take over as the croupier or some such thing," supposed Nancy. Percy struggled to envisage their entry into a casino let alone seamlessly taking control of the Black Jack table.

"We'll use make up and disguise. You can be an elderly man in a wheelchair and I'll be your glamourous carer or young wife," she said as she unzipped a make-up bag and brought out an item.

"Nancy it's an eyebrow pencil not a magic wand," he said.

"Not sure if you're on board with this Percy? You're not a natural, are you?" she said with enough petulance for Percy to know he was being insulted. Mostly, he wasn't sure.

"Where there's a will, there's a way," she assured.

"Not always. Unfortunately," sighed Percy.

"We will try somehow to get the money and plan this trip," said Nancy wondering whether she sounded like some tea drinking Bolshevik. "It's hardly a revolution…just a holiday."

And Percy led the way back into the kitchen through the French doors wondering where the three of them might go on holiday.

And with those seeds sown and the plan to make-a-plan in hand they ended their visit with their usual ritualistic custom. Both took a banana out of the wooden fruit bowl and split it in two and exchanged halves.

As soon as Percy left, Nancy patted up the wooden staircase thinking how best to make herself look eighteen. With each step a new thought struck her. Which lipstick? Which eye shadow? Red and green maybe? And her mum's clothes…which could she wear? The shoes were going to pose a problem as her feet were only size 3? These thoughts tantalized her, and at the top of the stairs, she thought she could at least try to pass herself off as adult, be it a rather small one.

It was a familiar sight, just in a new setting, her mother's dressing table was by far the most shi shi item in the house. There it stood, spread with an array of wonders. The gilded handled mirror on the dresser which enabled images of both front and back, evoked flashes of a mother and daughter, each with French plaits and matching faces. Her mother's scent permeated the air.

She plonked herself on the same comfortable sagging chair placing the chintzy cushion under her bottom to give herself some added height. With relish Nancy threw open the drawer which revealed an odyssey of make up through the ages. Some of which, Nancy surmised, was well past its sell-by date. She would have to remind her mother of all that lead poisoning that the ladies at court died from in the Tudor court. There were bound to be parallels.

There took place a great deal of squirting and rubbing and face pulling and general experimentation before Nancy concluded her eyes looked good in both green and blue eyeshadow. She avoided the temptation to do one in each colour.

"Tiger, Tiger, Burning Bright," she said, admiring her made-up eyes. Nancy put on her mother's music and whilst trying on lipsticks joined Blondie on the vocals, *One way or another*. And took a selfie.

Elated and determined with chin raised and gaze fixed, she took another photo hoping to show Percy he'd been a Doubting Thomas. Surely it was possible to acquire fake ID to gain entry to a Casino to win enough money to take your mother on an exotic holiday? Why limit yourself? You could save *the middle way* for later.

Nancy might not have *a sword by her side or Homer in her pocket* but she did have high hopes and intended to fulfil those whose measure she was up to. She might not make Australia but she'd enjoy trying.

Chapter 9
The Club

Over the next few weeks, several schemes came and went in Nancy's head, as one faded another would start crystallizing. She wanted to expand her sphere of influence.

She'd taken to Percy very strongly but his time was limited. At weekends, he was often off somewhere with his family of a hundred and one uncles. And week days, more and more his parents called upon him to amuse his younger sister.

Recently, Mrs Baskerville, wholly against her preference, was required to work from home.

"Are you sure the office is actually closed and it's not just her they've sent home?" Nancy had asked but seeing Percy's expression quickly added. "Because they knew she had a young child and thought it might help with the work/life balance."

Percy let the comment go and said, "I'm the one keeping Ada amused now that she's spending less time at the childminders."

"Well I would have loved to have a big brother like you?" Nancy had said quite certain Percy would be a total asset as a sibling, no matter the birth order.

She still counted her blessings on having had the good fortune to meet Percy at all. Before him, Nancy had never created any such an attachment outside the family: her family of two.

Previously, she'd maintained a safety-in-numbers approach, flourishing on a wide assortment of companions to meet various needs: a theory now challenged. *Variety is the spice of life* might be alright for some, but when you discover you prefer salt things change. These days Nancy wanted to spend time with Percy: and as with salt wanted him with everything.

"If the salt's not there what d'ya have to do?" she asked herself thinking back wistfully to an earlier time when she possessed an ability to self-partner and was able to make herself chuckle. Now she felt two's better, especially a confluent duo, like her and Perc.

However, in its absence she'd go for numbers…take up the tried and tested, *the more the merrier* approach.

On Friday evenings, Fern attended a Pilates class which was usually followed by drinks shared between the inner core practitioners, at the village pub. This was followed by a stagey, apologetic entrance by Fern returning through the front door, after a shaky key action, outstretching her arms in saccharine annoying affection, raving about her new friends and trying to squeeze Nancy like a rag doll. Fern was a woman who made friends easily, and ditched them too.
"Life's just an ever-changing series of dance partners for some," Nancy once told her stiffening as she wriggled free.

On this particular evening the fact that she was home alone rankered Nancy more than usual. Before Fern had taken up Pilates they had snuggled up on the sofa on Friday evenings. They'd dance around the kitchen to *Florence and the Machine* or Indy sounds. Make ridiculously large and unhealthy snacks! Then take these giant snack-filled bowls and bury themselves beneath blankets to watch Netflix films, the content way above Nancy's age limit.

Maybe if that still went on she wouldn't have cared two hoots.

Nancy even regretted so rigorously refusing to join Miss Trott's netball team. She could see its attraction now. They had an away match Saturday morning. She had nothing planned. Nothing planned Sunday either.

It was in this frame of mind, during this protracted weekend, that Nancy decided to join a club. She pounded her phone and scoured the local guides but saw no obvious fit. Nothing. It was fixed in the stars that she would have to create her own club. In no time one had sprung from her young mind. It would include three treasured ingredients: Fresh air and fun and all importantly, dogs.

A club had to have a name and the pretentious name she came up with was *The Young Jaunters* though she was aware it might alienate some. As Abraham Lincoln had once struggled with his man and property dilemma she wasn't yet able to

successfully tackle the thorny topic of dog ownership. As yet. She wanted fun and access to dogs, not political headaches.
The club was to meet on alternate Saturday mornings and its base would be the village green or her garden, depending on numbers.

They would go on japes with as many dogs as possible. And in Nancy's world: *four legs were better than two.*

Nancy knew food was important as the young, too, very much *march on their stomachs*. Members would be encouraged to bring food their own. She didn't envisage any problems with litter. It went hand in hand with potty training. Even Ada, a selfish madam, could identify the correct bin to put an apple or a scribble-picture that did not please her.

There was bound to be an abundance of food. With the exception of the waif-like Amy Fairweather-Coutt, everyone at school would go for the picnic. Nancy imagined Amy, as a foxhound crossed with an Italian greyhound with an exquisite I'm sure look on its face. She couldn't decide whether it would be a blessing or a curse to have **her** a member of the club.

Sunday was spent straightening out the details. In a way, Nancy was glad she'd not been disturbed by Fern who'd been in bed all morning or by Percy who'd gone out to yet another National Trust Property with his family and Uncle Bob.

Nancy felt Jaunt club was a worthy idea. It was emerging now to be a two-pronged affair. And it was to be exclusive. By invitation only.
Her mind ran rampant. She conjured a mental image of Percy, dressed up as a fox with select class mates in mock hunting gear on hobby horses, careering after him. Prizes. Fun. Food. All things fabulous would avail. They would be awash with laughter. It would emphasize a great deal of exploration. They'd ramble, mad with abandonment. Gayly sprint from spinney to brook.

The second prong would involve actual dogs. This aspect would have direct bearing on the invitations she planned to dish out that very Monday.

Nancy peeped out from behind her blue bedroom curtains to look out on the blanket of green turf below. Her mind's eye envisaged it abrim with activity, like some Spanish square or London park, a swirl of folk and dogs of all shapes, colour and size.

Through the twilight, her eyes trailed towards the attractive sea green of the garden shed and there she saw a fancy club house and in the ebbing evening a tinge of excitement trickled through her system spreading across her face in a broad smile. Before turning the light out on this peculiarly lonesome, if productive week-end, Nancy felt a violent urge to share this new idea with Percy. But as she messaged him she became aware that there were issues of practicality and maybe she should iron them out before making him party to her plan.

So instead she reverted to their old game of matching class mates with dog breeds. This had started with the teachers but had soon run out.

"Alison Shuttleworth, dog type?" she texted. Percy, nimble with his thumbs, shot back...*Small triangular head...steps out smartly Prussian solider style…shiny black and tan coat…high head carriage and tall for a terrier of slight build eyes bright to the point of beady…two pricked ears, isoscelesque. One might think it the product of a 1930's fascist and an absconded ballerina"*

"Manchester Terrier?" concluded Nancy.

"On the cold wet nose!" texted Percy.

She thought Percy on fire and wondered what had gone on that day at Compton Verney.

"Percy you're sparkling like a glass of Veuve du Cliquot at its finest rather than your usual half a cider, half-drunk, and discarded by a bored date at a suburban pub."

She wanted very much to meet this uncle of Percy's and made a note to ask if he were a military man.

"Not a kind girl always, are you Nancy?" texted back Percy who was thoroughly tickled.

Nancy sent back a heart.

She counted her many blessings as she looked at the glass of water on her bedside table, stared at its clear freshness, and thought it very much more than half full. She lapped at it. Her cup brimmeth over she decided as some droplets flicked her cheeks.

She climbed into her bed puffing up her pale blue pillows behind her but didn't feel tired. It wasn't Wifi cut off for Percy until nine, so she rang him.
"The canine counterpart of Emma Fothergill?" Nancy didn't wait very long for an answer.
"Pug," said Nancy as if it was a foregone conclusion. "Eyes bulging tongue panting dribbling down its squashed overbred face – stubborn mindset, positively porcine."
"She does slobber a bit," Percy, rarely exposed to such plain talking, wondered if it was PC, but he had to agree.
"Well it's not her fault," said Nancy "I mean maybe her tongue is too big for her mouth like James 1st and that Holy Roman Empire Hapsburg lot."
"Pugs have their redeeming features, they're sort of solid and square," said Percy. "Oliver Cromwell had one."
"Ah that might explain their round heads. Josephine had one too," said Nancy.
"A round head?" said Percy.

"Yes. Pugs before they had their noses bred off," said Nancy.

"Funny to think of the Cavaliers and their long hair with their fancy Cavalier King Charles spaniels with their long silky ears," said Percy.

"I wonder what they'd think of the Cockapoo," She had an image of the empress Josephine lying on a luxurious bed somewhere with her dear pug waiting. She'd heard that Josephine, though very beguiling, had no teeth so she gave the pug an overbite to compensate.

"Oh, they'd love them. Who wouldn't?" said Percy.

Nancy was completely unsure now in her previous leaning to the conclusion that Percy was an obvious match for a champagne coloured cockerpoo and considered maybe there was more to it.

She had classified herself in the early days as a beagle but with a tail more upright than standard, proud but not gone over, but now she realized that the match was all wrong and was fabricating a canine history for herself that involved so many countries and breeds that it would have to be written down. She was a mongrel with an extensive and diverse pedigree spanning four continents at least.

"Well on one thing we both agree is that your good friend Will would be a Springer Spaniel. Good night Perc and I want to hear more about your weekend in the morning," said Nancy and left Percy with the image of his classroom pal, William Cotton, on all fours chasing a ball.

Once Nancy's head hit the pillow she thought of her club idea again and conjured dreams of canine frolics through bucolic lands and picnics spread across a bluebell dell. A place of bonhominee, camaderie and general joie-de-vivre. Games of hide and seek. Some two-sided ventures creating a little tension but complimented by no stress bridge building exploits.

Most of the time would be spent in exploration climbing in and out of haybales, swinging on gates and gate flipping, paddling in brooks with the occasional boost of jumping in and off tractors…joy riding willing donkeys, climbing hills and other elevating pursuits. She continued to devise ground rules to the time-honoured game of hide-and-seek. She would divide them and adjudicate according to their aptitude and canine companion.

No one would feel slighted as she considered herself a super empath and might use a decision-making coin or just let the dogs choose.

***

When the children met at their usual spot on Monday morning Nancy listened with great interest to Percy's excursion to Blenheim Palace and added some key points to Percy's understanding of this fine Stately Home. They decided they were both in awe of the Marlboroughs.

"My Uncle Ben said that the Duke, though the richest man in the land, didn't dot his *i*'s to save expense on ink," said Percy.

Nancy looked at Percy rounding her eyes. She liked to be kept abreast of the affaires of Percy's Uncle Ben, who was quite often present on such outings. Though she'd never met him, she felt she liked him very much.

Spring had gained traction and pushed out colourful tulips to join the fading sheets of cream and yellow daffodils around the village. The Ides of March had come and gone, leaving offerings of crocuses, orange and purple. The scent of hyacinth wafted in the air. Neither the colour, nor the delicious aroma was lost on them.

As the two children, dressed in their fresh Monday morning school uniforms turned the corner into Colombine Walk, Nancy could keep it to herself no longer and splurged her club idea out.

"My mate Will Cotton's been put on this good earth to chase balls and the obsession shows no signs of abating. Its Ok for a bit but when I'm around his house **all** he wants to do is play football. I mean I do quite like a kick about but..." Percy's voice trailed off.
"Sounds like tunnel vision. Never takes an eye off the ball? We did have him down as a Springer. They're pretty hard-wired," said Nancy.
"Yes, he is, my aunt's Labradoodle is the same... just loves balls," said Percy.
"I suppose there's always ball aversion treatment," said Nancy.

Percy didn't like to think of that and was sure his parents wouldn't approve of it.

"In my club," Nancy announced, "They'll be no ball games."

Percy was not particularly fond of the No word. He thought that might be harsh and didn't quite know what she was on about.

Nancy reaffirmed, "In my club there is no room for flirtation on this matter."

"What club?" said Percy.

"It's a club where members are joined by invitation only, and you are invited," said Nancy.

"Is it a club if there are only two of you," said Percy.

"Most certainly…ultra-exclusive but we will grow it Percy. Look out for recruits. We can discuss their suitability. Is there any one in your class with or closely connected to a Saluki, Great Dane or Irish Wolf Hound?"

Percy didn't think there was. He still didn't know what she was on about.

"Lurcher?" said Nancy.

"Are we to include anyone not in class 5 or 6?" he asked.

"Why limit ourselves" said Nancy as they came to the end of Colombine Walk and turned into Fishpond's Road.

"We're looking for locals – we don't want parents involved in lifts and no one under eight," she said.
"So not a complete open door," he said.
"Is there ever such a thing?" said Nancy.
"Maybe once in the very beginning," said Percy.
"Such an old head on such young shoulders," said Nancy. "How very Anubic. Who could beat a god dog?"
Percy felt chuffed as he'd never been likened to a Jackal before. He thought them quite cool.

Chapter 10
A Day Out

And as time went by and Spring blossomed into Summer so, too, did the friendship between Percy and Nancy. This hadn't grown from seed or bulb. When Nancy met Percy, there had sprung forth such natural affinity it was as if two sides of a walnut clicked together to form one. Under this tough barrier existed all the complicated topography of the human brain. These two halves, encased cozily, felt equally at home.

Nancy still had it in mind to start a club and partly to this end, was trying out footpaths. That Saturday morning, she welcomed the sight of Percy coming in through the back gate. He found her in a heightened mood.
"We must all run in wild zigzags across fields of green," she announced.
"Mmm," said Percy almost certain that the code of conduct was to stick to the paths.
"For the club idea we can go to a high point and map out our territory like they did in Swallows and Amazons. The land will speak to us and conjure up names. The characters in Swallows and

Amazons spoke of; *Unexplored Artic, Rio, High Greenland, Wild cat island* and *Octopus lagoon*."
"I'm not sure if the kids round here would buy Octopus lagoon. They're a bit more informed these days," remarked Percy, who net-checked everything. "Blue Planet and all that."

Nancy fluttered her eyelashes and directed the whites of her eyes to the sky above declaring in a murmur something about age and cynicism.
"We will adapt," said Nancy who was deeply intrigued by the Octopus family with its eight-legged march through evolution, adjacent but very different from her own, split ever since the flat worm their humble common ancestor.
"There was talk of an escaped Puma. Its tail was meant to be far too long for an ordinary cat," said Percy. "And I know this man who says that in our parts, we have a highly unusual variety of fox.: the long-legged fox."
"Percy you are a genius. We can refer to Eoves Wood as Fox Island," said Nancy.

Percy smiled, though couldn't figure how it could be an island, as it wasn't surrounded by water. Also, he was wondering if Nancy was becoming a little swallowed up by ideology. He just wasn't up to playing Stalin to her Lenin, not that there was anything brutal about the club at this stage.

"We'll caper too," added Nancy.

Percy nodded his head. He wasn't exactly sure what it entailed but it sounded harmless enough.

"We'll run against the wind Perc," said Nancy giving his thigh a squeeze. "Have you any fairy-lights? We should do up the garden shed. It can be our headquarters…our club house?"

"Uncle Bob might have some," said Percy.

"Yes, I rather hoped he might. Come and choose your treats?" said Nancy advancing to the kitchen.

"Can't beat a Double Decker," he said popping one into his bag along with a packet of Salt and Vinegar crisps. Nancy packed the peanut butter and jam sandwiches in hers and then proceeded to successfully juggle satsumas before chucking one gently at him. To his astonishment he caught it and with his left hand. His right was full of fig rolls.

He marvelled at his good fortune and couldn't think of another person with which he felt so much rapport.

And so, they set off on this early summer's day equipped with snacks and hearts held high.

Their exploration for suitable hikes led them deep within this rural idyll.

The pasture was glorious that summer. Waist-high grasses and thistles rocked in the greenery, wafting delicious summer scents. Meadow Browns, Peacocks and Green-veined whites adorned the vegetation in a kaleidoscope of fluttering colour. After acutely observing their busy proboscises Nancy delighted herself in mimicking their sucking motion as she explained to Percy the main differences between Moths and Butterflies.

Maybe it was her unfilled dreams of being a pony owner, frustration at never having a chance to ride or the general killing calmness of the summer's quiet, we don't know. Whether or not it was a spur of the moment thing or a long-held ambition Percy wasn't sure, but when Nancy got up from the shade of their spreading oak Percy could tell that she was up to something. He could see her surveying cows like the Romans might have possible city states to plunder.

Nancy chose her cow on two main points. Number One, it looked a gentle animal and

Number Two, it was away from the others. Whether this cow was a claustrophobic, or anti-social or had just been sent to Coventry for some reason I can't tell you but it was a good distance away from the rest of the herd.

A nimble being with a good deal of spring, Nancy approached like a cat. She lowered her body and took long but very quiet steps and stalked it so calmly the cow didn't take much notice. Then its black and white head jerked up. Still chewing, it looked on the verge of panic.

Nancy went 180 degrees and ran at it, threw herself over its back and quickly scrabbled her leg over. Ha! She was on its back and a smile of triumph spread across her face like jam on a buttered scone.

The cow wasn't having any of it and Percy had some sympathy for it. It swung round dropping its head and bucked Nancy off in seconds. Nancy's landing was soft, avoiding both cow dung and thistles. Percy was horrified and excited in equal measure.
"Nancy you rode a cow," he said.

"Mmm, my approach was all wrong but we just don't have time in this life to do everything right," she said.

"I'll remember that one," said Percy following her back to the gate.

They made their way along the brook back to the village.

"Your house or mine?" asked Percy when they reached the green.

"Yours," said Nancy.

"Shall we go and slide down some bannisters?" suggested Percy.

"Then some checks and balances…on the sea-saw," said Nancy

"Reach for the stars my friend," said Percy.

Percy's back garden was as wide as it was long. It was sparsely planted. A Forsythia was fading pale yellow along the rear fence and a Cyananthus sat forlorn and blue in a barked border along with a couple more bushes that Nancy didn't recognise they reminded her of Japanese prisoners of war in small bamboo cages trapped on the side lines of a brutal war.

Not wanting to go inside on this sunny day she sat on the patio then turned her face to Percy and panted. Percy disappeared into the house

returning with two glasses of apple juice. He'd been quite surprised by its presence as he'd opened the large fridge to get chilled water. He figured his dad must have done the shopping.
"What would be your perfect dog?" he asked as he made his way back to the garden table and with unsteady hands placed the drinks down.
"Wild and yellow" said Nancy. "Ears big and pointed and faithful, very faithful."
Percy stroked his ear lobe.
Then she dropped her head to one side adding, "I used to want the most beautiful Harlequin Great Dane but society stamped on that dream."
Nancy could still recall with vivid clarity the time, long ago, when Fern had put her foot down.
"If we ever did get a dog it will be a small and easy breed." Nancy had been five and it was one of the few times her mother had told her to manage her expectations. Nancy had toned down her bedtime dream there and then for a while. The Great Dane shrunk, lost its piebaldness and loose tipped ears and turned yellow. The new vision was of slighter build, long legged but medium sized, with fiercely erect ears and beautiful white canine teeth and a delicate pink tongue and could easily fit into the car.

It was this dog she described to Percy as they sipped their juice.

"Back to mine?" said Nancy as she heard a car pull into the drive.

The two of them plonked their plates into the dishwasher and sped out of the front door laughing.

"Still time for Morning Make believe," said Nancy looking at her watch that said two thirty.

She dragged him over to the dressing up box. It was mainly filled with Fern's old going out clothes but did have a Bowler and some other classic pieces.

"We're in Marbella. Who are you?" she turned with a piece of Spanish lace draped over her head, dangling over her forehead.

"Could I be a Spanish Waterdog?" said Percy on all fours panting, showing a pink tongue.

"Love it that the Obama's picked one as their family dog. Just imagine you had been in the same litter as it. You could have said I've got a brother in the Whitehouse…but no Percy not today," said Nancy.

Percy got up from all fours.

"For I'm Contessa Jacasta of Seville and I'm in need of a suitor. I'm the ambassador from the royal court of Isabella of Castille. She supported Christopher Columbus," said Nancy.

"So, we're around 1492 …Columbus sailed the ocean blue," said Percy. "He never ever got to the US, did he?"

"Should have turned left at Barbados," said Nancy.

"Apparently one time he got to the top of the roaring mouth of the Orinoco and still felt the fear in his skin… thought his ship would capsize," said Percy.

"Those caravels were tiny…Santa Maria sank," said Nancy. "Thought he might be in the Sea of Scotland…or Eden …as in Heaven! Poor lamb. He was miles off. Some people have such blind belief."

"Quite so, Nancy. You get a sense of this unassailable self-belief," said Percy.

"Bit like your mum," said Nancy and started laughing. "Helpful I suppose at times. Blind ambition."

"Makes me tired, to think of it," said Percy.

"Well dress up then Perc. Do you want to be Columbus or how about Velaquez?"

Percy foraged in the dressing up chest, made of handsome oak with brass fittings and very much lent gravitas to the occasion though looked a little incongruous on the kitchen floor next to the washing machine.

"I shall be Paaaablooo," said Perc warming to the idea.

"Great friend of the *Bloomsberries* I believe Percy," said Nancy.

"Well that's thrown some chiaroscuro on the morning," said Percy

"Back in five," said Nancy leaving the kitchen to race upstairs and rummage through her mother's make up.

She plonked down in front of the mirror and with a lipstick in one hand bent forward, pursing her lips between applications and then wiped some off with a wet one before reapplying. She felt Perc was missing out.

All Percy had found to put on was a back to front man's white shirt, a beret and a tooth brush. He was sitting in the lounge when he heard a noise in the kitchen.

On opening the door all he could see was Nancy's bottom as she bent over the chest. She stood upright, turned her wig bedecked head and

purred in an accent of a Russian Blue, "No es Paaaablo."
How silky her voice thought Percy.

She approached the boy who held a toothbrush in one hand and a beret on his head with the other. She shimmied towards him and large chunks of brown hair fell in heavy coils to her waist. She had black lace that fell on both sides of her face. The makeshift symmetry was balanced to perfection.

"Es Salva-dor…Dali, Darlink!" said Nancy leaning forward with a black eyeliner pencil embellishing Percy's sweet face with a long thin, twirling moustache.
"I think you've inherited your philtrum from your mother. It's an art," she said, reading the wonder on the small boy's face.

Nancy looked him over and dimmed her smile.
"Take my photo, would you?" she asked.
"We are on the Aviendo del Mar…just down from the Playa de Venus. Let us just bump into each other. Put some chunk in your chihuahua Perc."
"Hola," he managed, trying to block out the far from Spanish feel of the thoroughly English lounge.

"Signor! The inquisition is at hand," She cried grabbing his hand.

Percy looked so alarmed it made Nancy burst out laughing.

"Oh Perc…shall we call it a morning?" she managed sitting next to him on the sofa.

"I think reading about Guernica's unsettled me," he said. "The world is such a mean place. It all gets so nasty. So tribal…and all that my obvious enemy is my friend if they are an enemy of my enemy."

"Oh," said Nancy "Stop there. Lord love us and save us. We're on a play date. Lord have mercy on our souls," Nancy said throwing her eyes up to the ceiling and flicking her brown tresses here and there.

"You could do with a fan in that outfit," suggested Percy. "I'll buy you one when we go on holiday next."

"You did have a point Perc," said Nancy sitting down next to him just an inch away.

"War and all that. It is just a good few spots short of a Dalmation, in'it."

Percy let out a deep breath signalling total agreement.

"Shall we eat biscuits?" she suggested.

Once back in the kitchen Nancy took off her extremely large wig and the excitement of the morning started to wear off.

"Fig roll Percy?" offered Nancy brightly.

"Yes please," he said.

"Take two. One for you and one for your biome," said Nancy.

"And that Franco…1939-1975 or something like that?" started Percy.

"Get your foot off my neck…" said Nancy, "You should never hold your Pomeranian on too short a lead."

Percy, gorged by passion, smiled.

Chapter 11
Invitation

A while had elapsed since Nancy's grand vision for a club. But on Monday morning she pinned her Jaunt Club invitation to the class noticeboard. It looked good. They'd used Mrs Baskervilles home/work printer.

There was a border to the A5 card Percy had designed with an assortment of dogs and a picture of the back of two figures with small rucksacks walking together amidst the Malverns. Nancy thought his choice of dogs a little lacking but understood he'd had to use what was readily available. Overall the design was very good. She'd stipulated the lettering must stand out.
"It must beckon, Perc. Beckon," she'd enthused.

They agreed to go for the more the merrier approach but to trial it first in her class. She was hoping for a good turn up.

Certain individuals huddled around the invitation and comments were made loosely.
"Oh, I don't fancy that," said Abigail.
"I have riding lessons every Saturday," said Lily.

There was a bit more of a shuffle but then everyone took their places and lessons began. This was taking an unexpected turn. Nancy wondered if she should sell it more but decided it was better to just wait and see.

By Wednesday they had had just one candidate and even he wasn't sure.
"I **might** be able to get Bouncer," he'd said.

This had lent a flicker of hope for the project until it was ascertained Bouncer was a Maltese terrier who lived with the boy's gran in Liverpool.

Nancy was surprised at how set-back she was by the whole thing. She felt not only on the back foot but lamed. Was the effort worth it?
"I'm not as robust as I thought," she admitted to Percy as she dragged herself back from school that day.

By the end of the week, she'd all but given up on the idea of the dog themed Jaunt club, resorting to the game of doggy-double.

On the way out of school she whispered to Percy. "Corgi," as they passed out of ear shot to Devak.

"Dalmatian," she said as they passed Ella Gardiner.
"I'm not sure if Ella would like to be known as a dalmatian," said Percy as they reached the street. "She may never need to know, now that the club is unlikely. Besides there's a lot of athletic ability in the breed. They were carriage dogs… bred to run miles. She'd have cut such a dash running behind the slay. If Ella didn't want to be a dalmatian she wouldn't have had to. They say be nice to everyone on the way up blah, blah, blah."
"Yes," agreed Percy. "On that illuminating reminder of the escalators and lifts of time,"
"Oh, indeed this mortal coil," replied Nancy.

It was a *dog fortnight* before the cloak of inspiration covered Nancy yet again and licked her face. This time, there wasn't actually a hint of the dog about it. The idea was a time-honoured one and still half-baked. It was to form a tuck shop, of sorts. Nancy ran the idea of a Noodle bar past her mother. She'd said, "Turnover vanity Profit Sanity."

Fern was used to getting these fancies from her daughter. She called them 'fads'. Nancy would get an idea and suddenly everything else was submerged to it.

At eighteen months old Nancy had suddenly acquired the predilection by various means of collecting all cushions available and lining them up. Then she would change the order on account of size, colour or design as if hanging Old Masters at the Uffizzi.

One minute, Tiger Cushion was central and then there was a reset and it had been flung back on the sofa in clear surplus, in its place the orange one bearing Winnie-the-Pooh.
"It's like watching the Prime Minister in a Cabinet reshuffle," Fern once confided to a friend.

There would be a line of them, two round turquoise ones either side, on one end book marked by the oblong cushion with the Scottish terrier tapestry and on the other end a pink pillow from the bedroom.

Nancy would bottom shuffle back to gain perspective and make the necessary adjustments. The next month she couldn't care less about cushions and was on to the vegetable rack and fruit bowl creating pleasing forms, at least to her, and according to Fern created colour combos that Matisse would have been proud of.

Fern remembered this fad fondly. It had been during their caravan years on the Yorkshire Moors. Nancy was very proud she'd spent some of her formative years in such a hallowed and romantic landscape.
"Wild and precious," she'd told Percy. "I heard that phrase in the film NYAD."
"And what will you do with your wild and precious life?"

"Wouldn't sandwiches be easier," Fern said but paid more attention when she deemed a semi-plausible monetary opportunity present.
"Nancy's one for the side Hustle," she later confided in a friend.
"Mum you are so not with the…" Nancy had said.
"Programme," finished Fern who thought she was pretty tuned in compared to some.
"Don't you have to cook Noodles?" she asked her daughter.
"Yes, but anyone can bring sandwiches to school. That's the USP. Unique Selling Point. Hot at the

point of access," explained Nancy her enthusiasm re-inflating.

"I'm sorry Nancy. It's not something I can get behind," she delivered her verdict firmly but kindly, adding. "I have to take Herman to the garage now. The MOT's out."

"Why do you always leave it so late?" Nancy said. "Poor forward planning…all round issues around organisation…" Fern's voice trailed off as she strode down the garden path, alongside the fabulously coloured pansies.

By the time Fern had crunched her way down the garden path she had thrown out the worrisome mental image of her daughter wielding a Calor gas cannister in some out-of-bounds maintenance shed.

Nancy, though no mechanic, had detected trouble with the Power steering and feared this might very probably impact on *Herman*'s road worthiness. He would fail the MOT no matter what regalia Fern had adorned him in. She'd better not lose another job because of it.

Percy was waiting in their usual spot when Nancy appeared.

"What about?" she said and took several steps alongside him to give him a chance to guess. "An Ice-cream palour!" she shouted and jumped up and down. "Imagine far east corner of the playground, an elegant round table with two long stools," Nancy flung her arms wide. "On it sit two knickerbocker glories piled high with ice-cream and each of those delicious scoops of Cornish ice-cream topped by the *glaciness* of the sweet red cherry and this cool mixture inserted with colourful straws...maybe a zigzag of chocolate piping."

Percy approved until reality set in.

"We'll wangle a freezer. Is your dad a member of Lion's?" she asked.

Percy shook his head.

"Good job there's Gum tree!" said Nancy.

Even though he wasn't at his best that early in the morning to give him his due, Percy had worked out how many they would have to sell with a hundred per cent mark up.

By home time Nancy's imaginings were spiraling. "We could run a clandestine Home Bar, Percy," she said. "The modern-day equivalent to a Sixteenth Century Smoke house or Seventeenth

Century coffee house, where people come to enlighten themselves. We'd decorate the walls with italic black ink, words of Wisdom. We could do kid's homework… for a fee. Provide ambience. Do juice, too. Shake all mocktails that contain fruit juices, others should be stirred," she informed Percy as they rounded the corner, Percy on the outside in true gentlemanly fashion.

"I've heard of those coffee shops in the old days…but smoking houses," said Percy.
"Yes, yes the men sobered up in them. And before coffee everyone was nuts for smoking. The infamous Jack Hawkins bought it back."
"Thought it was Walter Raleigh?" said Percy.
"My source says it was Jack the Slaver. Walter only popularized it at the Elizabethan court. Showed everyone how to fill their pipes. Very, very widespread. Apparently, Shakespeare was always puffing away. Though James 1st couldn't stand it."
"Well I've never heard of that," said Percy.
Nancy changed the subject back to Mocktails though she thought it might be interesting to see Langton Green Primary School all slightly tipsy from the first bell to home time.
"A jigger is a shot, six or seven drops," she said.

"La Planteur is divine." Nancy had always loved the banana, in fact she had a banana-shaped light in her bedroom next to a miniature complete works of Shakespeare with a case of sterling silver. They divided at the school gates.

Nancy wasn't finding her Mandarin easy that morning. There was a supply teacher who didn't know how to log her into her Year 8 Maths programme and Nancy had completed Year 5's lesson in three and a half minutes. To stave off boredom she'd taken to her Mandarin. Usually she could work around a certain level of hullaballoo but this morning it was too much.
"Well that's the thing," said Nancy later on that day as they were walking along Columbine Walk, "If you're not in with the in crowd there's no one to out you."
She was still mad at Year 5 for not being whole-heartedly stopped in their tracks and raring and woofing to go at her dog club. Had she been barking up the wrong tree to expect it? Could she be bothered to pee up another nine hundred and ninety-eight wrong trees?

Wasn't it, Napoleon, she asked herself, who hinted war was a series of misjudgements and winning fell to the powers that just made the fewest mistakes.

She was mad at Abigail Pullen-Thompson who had poured cold water in such an ugly manner. When it leaked out that Nancy wasn't doing Maths but Mandarin Abigail had shrugged her angular shoulders with a "I don't know why you bother it's all on translators now."
Nancy gave forth a small huff and raised her eyes to the ceiling.

Abigail and her sidekick Lily agreed together that Nancy was unlikely to ever get to China.
Nancy felt it was worth the effort on account that if she got a start now, when the plasticity of her neural synapses were stretchy and her transmitters were on fire, unlike a battery, the brain could store information therefore it was the real deal of making hay when the sun shone. And sometimes it wasn't where one goes but what comes to you.

Abigail Pull-The-Other one and Lily Lacky-Longlegs might find themselves to be linguistically ill-prepared if world order significantly shifted.

Nancy resolved to concentrate on the conversational pieces of Mandarin by way of cambio-exchange with Amy Tan. She needed to learn *F Off* for starters.

Lily and Abigail could join some others on the bench. She would relegate them to the furthest recess of her brain and there they must remain… not worth another thought.

Nancy understood that most of the class were decent enough and it wasn't so much that they didn't **like** her club but that they were already committed. Nancy had had a change of heart about ball games in general and now decided that they were indeed a very useful element of society…at least partly responsible for world peace.
"Everyone needed to shift a ball of some sort. It was when the ball stopped rolling the trouble set in," she told Miss McBride. Miss McBride agreed with her. She said the Mayans took the penalty thing a little further. Miss McBride was proving a very interesting woman. Nancy kept her growing admiration for this individual quiet from her

mother but was able to tell Percy who didn't have a jealous bone in his body.

Nancy picked up a lot from Miss McBride. They discussed Geo-politics with gusto in particular the countries involved in water wars.

Liking Miss McBride so, Nancy had adopted a quiet approach, keeping any sparkiness on a short rein. Intuitively she knew when to push a button and when to shut up and watch the reaction. During lessons she rarely spoke but when she did even the most disengaged person perked up to listen.

Nancy would amaze her teacher with her depth of knowledge and conciseness of her answer.
"You can ask her about anything?" Miss McBride would tell her partner Harvey.
"She probably just googles it," said Harvey who wasn't interested in school matters.
You haven't met her, thought Miss McBride.
"Speaks Mandarin. Can do an air somersault."
Why aren't I pregnant? How I want a little person? Soul mate. Future. She would act if she were in my position. Is it you or me Harvey? Should I go now or stay? It's my house. Where would you go?

Chapter 12
The Bus Ride

By Friday Nancy had hatched a Saturday adventure. They would catch a bus. Once aboard they'd sit down and close their eyes and count to one thousand and then get off. The adventure would be in navigating their return across country. Manifest destiny.

The next morning found them stood at the bus stop waiting for the Number 88. They took the back seat and tied on their blindfolds.
"Close your eyes Perc," said Nancy, proceeding to count softly and slowly. She reached a hundred. Percy elbowing her the while.
"Mum and Dad will worry," he said.
"Thought you said they've gone to Woodstock…Chill your beans…did they say you couldn't go on a bus?" Nancy was annoyed that her counting, laborious as it was, had been interrupted.

Nancy stopped at seven hundred and fifty as Percy was clearly in genuine distress, fidgeting from buttock to buttock.

Nancy had hoped they would dismount the bus still wearing their blindfolds but Percy had already removed his.

She persuaded him to let her put her hands on his shoulders and follow him down the aisle. Such was her trust in him but she hadn't quite factored in the drop from the bus to the ground. She buckled at the knees as she stepped off the bus on to the kerb and would have fallen if it hadn't been for the support of Percy. The bus driver got very shirty.

"I'm not happy," he complained "You could have had a nasty fall." He was thinking of the wretched forms he'd have to fill out and on line, too. "Haven't you ever been young?" said Nancy having the wit to whip off her blindfold, and shake her reddish ringlets that bounced around her heart-shaped face.

He melted a little and muttered something about taking care and having a nice day. Nancy considered it was a small victory as he'd been a real crank.

They sat on the wide grass verge laughing under a sky of cornflower blue. Nancy, from her earliest years, was used to walking through fields as the crow flies. Fern was an early protagonist of the Right-to-Roamers.

"Now to work on our tracking skills and let forth our **magnetic** sense of direction. If swifts can do twelve thousand miles I'm sure three or four won't be a problem," announced Nancy.

"Into the breach," said Percy noting Nancy's wide smile and all-round visible delight.

The fields either side of the remote bus stop didn't seem to him so inviting. A ginger cat appeared from under a hedge, glanced momentarily at them and ran off.

Nancy took stock of her bearings. Now the sky was clouding over but the air was fresh and the horizon wide.

"Such a shame we don't have a dog," said Nancy wistfully as she raised her hand above her eyes and looked far across the fields.

"Look for a gap in the hedge Percy," she said. There wasn't an obvious one. Nancy would have liked to crawl through it but agreed to walk on a bit until they came to a gate. Percy hoped it would be a public footpath but had no such luck. He stood back as Nancy flipped over its five wooden bars with an easy motion. Percy would have liked to spring over it in a one-handed Brad Pitt type action but he was not tall enough, nor yet strong enough to master that particular feat.

When they passed into the second field Nancy was horrified when she thought she recognised the church spire. The excitement seeped out of her like water from a ruptured paddling pool. However, she reminded herself it was still a pretty day and then she realized she didn't after all recognize the church tower as it had no cock-shaped weathervane on the top of its spire.
"The trouble with trespassing is there aren't any dogs," she said.
"Only the possibility of guard dogs," said Percy nervously.
"Oh, don't worry landowners wouldn't dare. It's not Mr Burns or the 18th Century. Might get an over excited collie but their bark's u*sually* bigger than their bite."
Percy seemed to be going particularly slowly. Even for Percy. He had never been a speedy walker but Nancy wasn't used to this latest

dawdling.

She sped up and when he didn't respond she called out *Cow's Tail*. He put his middle finger up and she strode on, in a pretend huff, thinking she would hide and then spring out at him.

Thus, a distance began to grow between them: each determined to go at their own pace. After around a quarter of an hour she stopped and hid herself behind a vast oak tree and waited for her prey.

A minute passed, then five minutes turned into ten and still no sign of Percy. Nancy began to get an uncomfortable feeling. It was a sinking of spirits. She picked up her pace gradually. Well he was bound to be around the next corner. When she didn't see him, she wondered whether he'd retraced his steps. Or had he circumnavigated her? "Oh, don't go all lone wolf on me Percy," she said out-loud and doubled back across the field.
At the next field she started to run and call his name.

He was bound to be around the next corner.

Nancy looked at her watch again. It was becoming a mystery…not a Scooby doo fun one but quite unsettling. She heard herself huff whilst sitting on the upturned tree stump. It was the loneliness, the worry. Poor Percy, he wasn't used to be being on his own. Not with a family like that. What could have happened? Then this horrible thought came into her mind "The Santa Maria" had sunk. Tragedies did happen.

She took a swig of water and continued her search. Occam's Razor… the most likely scenario was that he was near…or on his way back home. He was probably sat on a bench back at the village…at Langton Green eating Salt and Vinegar crisps. Nancy wished they were slurping drinks together and seeing who could spit the furthest. Should she go back or forward? What would happen if she got there first and he wasn't there? The fear, she felt it spread through her veins. Nancy found herself hurtling down some rapid: swirling in a whirlpool between two worlds.

All was quiet. She'd ask the next person she'd see. She'd knock on doors of any building that lay in her path. *Have you seen a smallish boy? About this high.*

A full hour went by. *What would his parents say? Isn't this just typical …one minute you're on top of the Ferris Wheel screaming with joy…then…*
"Percy," she yelled her words cutting through the valley.

That evening Nancy visited Percy in hospital. On seeing her, he shuffled up his mattress to realign himself. His face winced as he repositioned himself but he was clearly cheerful.
"You're just like a Springer Spaniel," said Nancy when she saw him sitting up in bed grinning.
"Yes, you've got innate ebullience Percy," she said fixing him with her stare, she arranged his pillows, before straightening up his bedside cabinet and helping herself to a satsuma.
"I don't think a Springer would have got himself concussed in a ditch," said Percy.
"You have a point there," agreed Nancy.
He lent forward to Nancy and whispered, "They only kept me in because of my mum. I've only got a twisted ankle and a broken bone in my foot. She was very suspicious and thinks I got in a car with someone I shouldn't have. As if?"
"We don't want this thing to go wide. My mum was suspicious, too," said Nancy. *"How did he get five miles? Cross country? Near Snodsbury,"*

mimicked Nancy. I don't like not being straight with her but we couldn't put her in the middle of this...party to a conspiracy."

"Are we in a conspiracy?" asked Percy.

"Yes, we are. And we had better stay in one. If they find out they might split us up," said Nancy. "Well your mum might try."

Nancy picked out another satsuma and methodically peeled it as Percy told her of nurse Belinda's life story. There were aspects to being in hospital that Percy clearly enjoyed.

The School got involved. They sent in a large bowl of fruit and a card signed by the whole of Year 6. Percy was asked if he'd feature in a special Safety Awareness assembly to be held at the school in conjunction with Community Police Officers.

"Could there ever be such an indignity?" commiserated Nancy on her next visit.

Perc nodded trying to block out recent invasions to his privacy bought about by a nurse just doing her job.

"Survival…sometimes comes at a price, I suppose," he confided.

Nancy visited each day for the three days of Percy's hospital stay. The last two times she came in with Mr Baskerville with whom she was becoming friendly, and now called Ed.

At home, Fern was being more attentive. *Bless*, thought Nancy as they ate popcorn and watched sitcoms in their pyjamas.

It had been scary. She'd overheard her mother talking to one of her girlfriends.
"Well he may never walk again. They didn't know whether he was going to gain consciousness. They're doing tests. They may have to move him to another hospital."

Now that the danger had subsided and Percy was in full recovery, what most struck Nancy was how stirred she'd been. It was as if the sky had unzipped mechanically lowering a long forearm extending slowly forth with a warning, wagging finger directly in front of her.

It had been such an odd feeling arriving back without him. She was so certain he'd have got home before her. She'd spent hours looking for him.

It must have been fun being found by a Labradoodle called Pearl, she pondered but remembered he'd been unconscious. Nancy wondered if the sensation of the cold nose on his cheek had woken him.

**Chapter 13
The Fair**

Two weeks later, Nancy and Percy sat opposite each other at the kitchen table sucking at juice boxes, eating biscuits. They discussed Percy's brush with death which soon evolved into matters of science and religion. The pair weren't able to fix on a plausible creation story or definitively rule out an after-life.

A teacher at Nancy's previous school had started her fascination with creation stories. Nancy told Percy the one about an Innuit girl who fed her fingers to the fishes. Percy happened to be nibbling a chocolate finger at the time and he listened with great interest.

"The differing origin stories of the Greek and Roman explains their different approach to colonial expansion." Nancy told Percy. "You see the Greeks believed you came up through the earth therefore **only** those born in that land could be Greek. However, the Romans were much more inclusive. A melting pot. Gave out citizenship far and wide. Romulus and Remus and the wolf

mother came in from the outside, bit like the Founding Fathers, I guess."
"Horrid Romans when you think how they wholescale genocidal slaughter of certain tribes of Ancient Briton. Would you like to come to the Mop with us as our guest?" asked Percy. "Dad wants to know."
"Love to come Perc," said Nancy. "Love a mop."

The Baskervilles picked Nancy up on Friday night, quite early. Mrs Baskerville complained when they had to park some distance away.

The sounds and smells grew as the Baskervilles and Nancy drew nearer.

"They're so fringey," she told Percy "I mean look at him. I bet he could tell a story," pointing to the individual in charge of The Cup and Saucer Ride. Percy didn't think he looked very wholesome and Mrs Baskerville was holding on to Ada so tightly that on this occasion he felt Ada had every right to cry.
"She can't run away to the circus. She's at one," said Nancy out of earshot as they were let on a ride by a rather daunting looking fair guy. "Ada is a handful," said Percy.

"She'll be married with a couple of children and living in Margate by the time she's 35," said Nancy nonchalantly.

Soon they were in a casket rising on the Ferris wheel. Ada's screams were fading. The whole of Stratford stretched out before them. Beneath their dangling legs stood Mr and Mrs Baskerville. Music drowned out Ada's protests that she *was* old enough to go on the ride. For a while, they were detached from it all, going around and around.

Percy and Nancy, with their seat swinging, jerked higher and higher becoming more and more distant to the rumblings below. Whilst ascending Percy became overwhelmed by a sudden contentment. He said, "Right now, Nance. There's no place on earth I'd rather be!"
On the fairground attraction they circled in the sky.

Then things slowed and there followed a bump, bump, bump.
"And the truth is, the descent down can be just as magnificent, Percy. It's just a question of adjustment," said Nancy smoothingly.

"Easy when there's no choice I suppose. You have to go with the flow," he said as they disembarked. His little sister ran towards him beating her fists against his thigh before she was hauled off by Mr Baskerville with an unusually sharp reprimand. "Be careful of your brother. He's only just come out of hospital."
This seemed to have the desired affect and Ada pulled free and scooted around behind Mrs Baskerville, who looked awkward and out of place at the fair.

Percy and Nancy shared a candyfloss as they continued to follow in the footsteps of the Baskervilles and the constant shenanigans of Ada.
"Byron had a daughter called Ada," said Nancy. "She was a coder…a computer whizz."
Percy eyed his little sister and thought that she had the requisite fire in her belly to roll far. He said nothing. Instead, he gazed at Nancy as she opened her mouth on the large pink mesh of candyfloss, enraptured by its sweetness.
"Percy," she said, her head turned to catch his eye and her lips stained bright pink.
"Yes?" said Percy.

"I think we should hold a Mocktail Party for a select few to toast your fortunate survival," said Nancy.

Percy was beginning to realize that Nancy would tire of a theme only for it to reappear down the line.

"Maybe call a Mocktail after me?" joked Percy.

"The Hit and Run…No, no The Percy Prevailer… No, no…I know, I know," Nancy blurted through a sea of giggles.

"Well out with it then," said Percy quite used to this hysteria.

"Well," said Nancy "You gotta emphasis the product…the ingredient…so how about this one."

Percy kept walking and braced himself waiting for Nancy's endless laughter to subside.

"The…" she managed with panache, "Perc-zest!"

Percy had to admit it had a ring.

"It's so in line with the average kid's obsession with all things spooky," said Nancy quite over her burst of mirth. "Possessed…PercZest! Get it?"

"I'm sure a Mocktail named after me will be most edifying," said Percy.

"Oh Perc," said Nancy, "It wouldn't surprise me if one day they didn't name a street after you…or a whole town."

"And you will have one, too," said Percy who felt his blood rise.

The parents had managed to veer Ada away from the most alarming rides. They stood at the Catch a Duck stand. As they bobbed up and down in the water the yellow plastic ducks appeared quite small to Nancy. Although she'd outgrown them, she enjoyed the sight of Ada swinging her bamboo stick in an ardent attempt to snag one. Mr Baskerville offered a helping hand but Ada kept snatching the pole back then shooting it into the air with so much vigour that even the laidback administrator got up from his chair muttering that it wasn't meant to take all day.

Nancy took hold of Percy's sleeve gently and pulled him a few steps away from the scene. When Ada finally managed to capture a duck, Nancy started a handclap. It was namely for Ada but really to Mr Baskerville for his patience. She whispered to Percy about parents being *our longterm allies* and coordinated this with a very approving look. Mrs Baskerville spotted a friend and wandered off from the group.

The harmony was short-lived because a further battle commenced. Ada didn't want a fluffy chipmunk or any of the prizes on offer. She wanted the duck she caught, Number 33.

At this point Nancy turned her back on the scene and walked off. Percy asked his dad if they could meet back at the Helter-Skelter at seven-thirty. Mr Baskerville holding his daughter firmly by the hand agreed and Ada's rigid little face was crossed with a smile as she waved her plastic duck triumphantly and quacked.

The fair was well attended and night-time was falling. In a few short minutes amidst the crowd they were sucked into a world of sound and smell. "One day, I would like a perfume named after me," announced Nancy. "It will be the scent of all the roses ever yet grown. Its hues will be champagne-orange, crème-caramel and burnt saffron dappled with the vibrant orange of the juiciest clementine. Once sniffed, some innocence will be forever lost but true Wisdom imbibed. It will be a heavenly scent, at once cloying, even demanding, but with such delicate intense pleasure tantalizing you from the very heights to float on…"

She shut up.
"Like a rose you want to smell forever," concluded Percy.
She looked at Percy before taking another mouthful of her pink mountain. He looked back at her and smiled.

When Nancy was dropped home, Fern seemed very pleased to see her. She'd prepared Spaghetti, Nancy's favourite. Nancy was still in the midst of the funfair with its music ringing in her ears. The living room seemed small and drab. Fern sucked up a strand of spaghetti very noisily to get her daughter back into their world.

Nancy sucked up a strand, the sauce flecking her cheeks and they laughed but it didn't stop Nancy feeling the possibility of getting a sibling was getting thinner and thinner as her mum didn't seem to have any sort of love life.

"When do you think we can get a dog?" Nancy blurted.
Fern flinched and let out a sigh, "As soon as we can Nance…you know I'd love to get you a dog."
"But when mum?"

Chapter 14
Fern

Saturday morning Nancy was home alone until Percy came knocking and she pulled him in. "Thought we could co-write a children's story based on animals for the BBC this morning," she said even before Percy had a chance to sit down. "Could do one about a Fox?" said Percy thinking of *The Fantastic Mr Fox*.

"Yes," brightened Nancy. "We could do one about a fox and a ferret… a feral ferret. The local gun for hire."
"Perhaps, it could fall in with some stoats…walk on the wild side," Percy added, putting his cap back to front. "Or would that be a bit *too Wind in the Willows*, in'it?"
"Oh, ride on the shoulders of giants," assured Nancy ignoring the cap thing. "Besides *Ferret Grise* is the natural star… mixes with Polecats, *sinc*s, and turns ermine in winter."
"Phh…is that an upgrade?" said Percy who liked the colour grey.
"How about Foxy Renard meeting Great Uncle Basil?" he asked.
"Basil?" said Nancy who by her tone clearly

hadn't a clue but it was tempered by a certain admiration for the name.

"Basil," she repeated but this time emphasising the *b* and rolling through the letters lingering on the a making the *s* as silky soft as possible, and inferring that anyone who could carry off such a name had to be given an ear."

"Basil Brush! Dad talks about him. He was a famous Fox, not a real fox, a puppet on the TV…"

"Word of the week?" Percy suddenly asked.

"Ah," smiled Nancy "Approchment, A-prossh-mont," she mouthed again in what Percy believed to be a perfect French accent and tried to copy it. "Don't tell me but do I detect a Loire Valley lisp?" Nancy jumped clasping her hands together in delight.

For the first time in his ten years Percy was aware that he was living up to someone's expectations. It felt good.

"Place of the week?" Nancy returned.

"Marbella," said Percy. His parents had been talking of holiday destinations over breakfast.

"Mar-BAY-YA," repeated Nancy clasping her hands together and doing a twirl before sitting back down.

"Overrated I believe, unless you're a drug lord.

Malaga is on the up," she said and then abruptly changed the subject.

"Have you noticed anything about Fern?" she asked Percy as she placed in front of him the biscuit tin half full with loose fig rolls, milk chocolate digestives and ginger nuts.

"No," said Percy momentarily downcast by the absence of the chocolate finger.

"Though," he paused before taking a bite into the round of his digestive. "She does seem quiet...I mean your mum...well she's quite exuberant usually." He chose his words thinking of his own mother who was all together a more measured type. "She seems rather ...droopy for Fern."

"I knew it," said Nancy. "She's stopped pulling faces and just talks about work, work, work. We need to cheer her up. What's the secret of a good week?"

"Treats?" suggested Percy.

"Yes, we need to top up the treats. If it works for the average cockerpoo it should work for mum!" said Nancy as though a weight had been lifted. Percy wasn't so sure.

"Really, Nancy...what you should be thinking of is more long term. You need to get her a permanent playmate," he stated.

"I guess if you're down you just have to turn up

the treats and get friends round," said Nancy leaping off her chair with joy and shrieked, "A surprise party!"

Percy lowered his eyebrows and pinned Nancy with such a serious look that Nancy sat back down and listened to what he was about to say.
"What Fern might respond to positively is a man. It's the human condition." said Percy. "Can she do Tinder?"
"Mmm," said Nancy "They've been a mixed blessing in the past but I think you're right. It's going to be more difficult than buying a few olives and pouring crisps into a dish."
"Or blowing up some party balloons," agreed Percy nodding his head. "Tricky thing getting the right match…balancing suitability with chemistry. What's her boss like? Assuming he's a man and that's the way she rolls."
"TIM," squealed Nancy. "He's about twenty years younger…must be dispiriting."
"Yes," said Percy. "It must be hard being an adult when the hierarchy is against you."
Nancy shrugged. "Rome wasn't built in a day. In fact, some might say it's a great shame it was built at all."

She put the lid on the biscuit tin to signify a change in direction.

Nancy decided there should be some serious swiping going on and when Fern returned from Saturday overtime Nancy made her a cup of tea and insisted she took a bubble bath. Fern emerged refreshed and changed into her *comfie*s and was sat down by her young daughter on the sofa for a talk.

"Mum you know you always feel sad when you see a horse in the field by itself… herd animals and all that?" Nancy asked.
"Nancy I'm fine. We've just had a busy time at work… too busy," said Fern.
"Liberties," they said together and started laughing.
"All work and no play…" reminded Nancy.
"Yeah. Yeah. I know all about dating apps. I'll get on it…" smiled Fern all together more cheerful.
"Yes. Get swiping. It's a numbers game, mummy," said Nancy who didn't believe in always waiting until someone felt they were ready.
"Nail yourself to the mast. Fortune favours the brave. Tinder is your *triangular* sail…well up to the endeavour. As long as you're aboard, mum,

you should make headway. If it goes wrong. Well, it's not as though that's never happened before. The winds will just blow us gently back down the stream," said Nancy.

"Merrily, merrily," said Fern and realising just how much she'd missed confiding in Nancy. "And what's with all this nautical stuff?

Chapter 15
Holiday

Nancy could hardly curb her excitement.
Something amazing was happening.
The Baskervilles were taking her on holiday. She was going to Spain. She was going to a hotel!
"Andalusia," she said over and over running up and down the stairs.

From the word go, Nancy spent every spare second learning Spanish and reading up on Spanish history.

"Mum, they had this Christian, Moors thing going on, like us…The Crusades…and it went on, *the Turks are at the gate* and all that," said Nancy.
"Oh, that's religion for you," said Fern who was never one to engage much on religion or politics.
"But I do know Richard the Lionheart because he was in the Robin Hood films.
"Do you know who his mother was?" asked Nancy.
 "I know his brother was John. His mother…not sure. If she's not Eygptian, Tudor, Victorian or Boudicca then no."

"Eleanor of Aquitaine…a woman who makes East Enders look tame," Nancy said.

Nancy who had a growing grip on hegemonic aspirations of the top European families tried a final tactic to engage her mother in some debate.

"Sir Francis Drake, hero or villain?"

"Psycho," said Fern.

"Ah. An interesting answer," said Nancy who like many had a quiet interest in biology and the so-called warrior gene.

In general, Fern had limited time for history factual or counterfactual.

"Don't like the **if** word," she told her daughter.

"Can't believe you're off to And-da-loooo-sia. The hotel looks amazing…a gorgeous swimming pool, too!"

When Nancy had first told her mother about the holiday offer her face had momentarily fallen before lighting up and being delighted for *her little red foxlet*.

It was true the two of them had seldom been apart and certainly never for a week.

When Nancy got back from school the next day there was a brand-new Cabin bag in the kitchen. Turquoise. Nancy flung her arms up round her mother.

***

Although the journey to Spain hadn't run at all smoothly Nancy had savoured every moment. When they arrived at the hotel she was star struck. "It's like being in a Kingdom!" she declared to the Baskervilles as her eyes drank in her palatial surrounding.

Nancy looked up at the splendour of the chandeliers, then cast her eyes down to the swirling grey patterns of the marbled floor that spread to wide stairs on one side, and to the shining twin elevators on the other. This sea of streaked marble also flowed forwards to the wide horse shoe of the beech reception desk where immaculately dressed staff stood upright tapping into their computers and smiling radiantly at the incoming guests.

"Footmen?" said Nancy as she entered in through wide dark wood and glass doors, remembering in days of old they were the dandies of the day.
"Porters," said Mrs Baskerville. "Can't see their real point now everyone has wheelies." She was clearly tired and still holding Ada on her bony hip. In Nancy's opinion the child was very capable of walking on her *own two*.

Securing their keys at the magnificent desk they took the elevator *en famille*. It was a delight to Nancy who was reminded of the lifts in the big Babar book the teacher had read to them in France. She would have liked to press the buttons but Mrs Baskerville had already done so. They alighted on the third floor and spilled out of the lift.

"Here's our room, Perc. Room 66," Nancy cried turning the key with ease.
"We're right next door," said Mr Baskerville wheeling both cases towards his wife who had Ada by the hand and was trying to work the lock with the other.
"You would have thought they'd have got those plastic cards by now," she snapped.

Entering the room Nancy marvelled, "A room all to ourselves…and such a pretty one." They propped their cases up by the wall and looked around.

"A bath and a shower! And a balcony with table and chairs!" cried Nancy in disbelief.

"Which bed do you want?" said Percy.

"This one," she said sat with a bounce on one admiring the bedside cabinet and reading lamp.

"Perfecto," she said and stood up.

"Let's unpack! And go swimming," she said lifting her case on to the bed, unzipped it all the way round and threw open the lid.

"Look what mum packed. Bless." She said holding up a pack of playing cards.

"Oh…shall we play something," said Percy who wasn't at all sure if he wanted to go down to the pool yet. He wanted to rest up a little after the journey.

"What do you want to play? Fifty-two card pick up?" Nancy asked.

"Ok," said Percy who hadn't played cards much and wasn't familiar with the game.

Up went the cards, shooting from Nancy's hands up to the ceiling in a circular motion. Nancy burst into laughter and patted the bed with glee. "I felt as jet propelled as a cuttlefish on a squirt," she squealed and lowered her voice dramatically, "There's one over there," she pointed.

Percy said little before he started to placidly pick up the cards.

"I think if you were a card you'd be the Five of spades…mmm maybe the Four," Nancy continued to laugh so much that there were tears forming in the corner of both eyes.

"Mm," said Percy "And I suppose you'd be the Queen?"

"Red or black, Perc?" said Nancy.

"Either. Couldn't choose. Alright, Queen of Diamonds," said Percy.

"And you can be King…" she said and was down on her knees helping him pick up the cards which were soon collected up, put away and forgotten.

"I'm surprised Mum didn't put Ada in with us," said Percy, feeling a new lease of life, jumped up and down on his bed.

Nancy looked a little hesitantly at him as he went up and down. She didn't like to dampen his high-spirits but he was bouncing very hard.

"I can't believe our balcony," she said "We can see the pool," and tilting her head upwards she added "and the sky, so blue and endless."

"It's not a sea view," said Percy rather disappointingly as he clamboured off the bed and followed her out to the balcony.

"It's fantastic here. Look at the pool! Let's go try it," she said and headed for the bathroom to put on her costume. Percy had never seen her in a swimsuit and thought the colour suited her. She started rolling up the new matching turquoise towel Fern had bought her.

"Oh, the hotel provides towels," said Percy smiling.

"But, I've got to recognize it on the sunbed," she laughed.

"Thought you couldn't sunbathe," said Percy.

"What being a Ginge?" said Nancy smiling and running her fingers through her auburn hair. Percy thought he'd never seen a prettier girl.

"Life's all about the shade, Perc. Got to turn yourself to the sun...but never overexpose..." she walked towards the door. "Unless, of course, you want to burrrrrn," she added over her shoulder.

They decided to use the stairs on the way down which cascaded down in a sweeping half circle. Once out by the pool they dropped their things on a couple of sun beds and made their way to the kidney shaped pool.

"Beguiling," she declared as she dipped a hand into the water and then like a flash she was in. Percy who was sitting with his calves immersed in the water agreed.

They both had to shield themselves from the splash made by two bigger boys who had plunged into the pool in unison. Nancy started her lengths.

Percy entered the pool at the shallow end where the boys immediately tried to involve him in a ball game.

Nancy though annoyed she hadn't been asked, took little notice.
"Is she your sister?" enquired the taller one.
Percy shook his head.
"You're Piggy," said the blond boy to Percy and chucked the ball way over Percy's head to his friend. Nancy saw the other one snigger. She heard them shout out, "Piggy!" several times. She'd read Lord of the Flies and knew it hadn't ended well.

Tossed on the horns of a dilemma, she swam past them hoping the boys would soon tire of taunting

Percy. She would swim a couple more lengths. Then, if need be, take action. In her book, in most cases, *two against one* just wasn't on.

But as she was swimming back she saw the blond boy throw the ball very hard at Percy who had not managed to extricate himself from the regrettable situation.
"You're meant to catch it, not stroke it," shouted the other boy.
"I'm not that good in the pool," said Percy.
"Can I play?" Nancy interjected and as the ball had bobbed towards her, she took hold of it.
"Possession 99% of the….and all that," she said smiling very sweetly.
"Thought that was an ice-cream," said the blond boy to his mate who started laughing.

The two boys were summoned by their parents and once again Nancy and Percy had the pool to themselves.

At lunch, Nancy was mesmerised by the quality of food, the linen table cloths and the attentiveness of the waiters. They called her Signorina and spoke back to her in Spanish, which they didn't do when

Mrs Baskerville tried to talk to them in their native tongue.

Possibly the seafood soup at lunch had not agreed with Mrs Baskerville's internal machinations or something else rendered her unwell. Unluckily for Mr Baskerville his wife felt very off-colour and went to lie down with a bowl in hand, presumably as some sort of sick receptacle.

Mr Baskerville, after a long motorway drive and delayed flight, was now in sole charge of a tired and truculent daughter. Ada, although now three, was loathe to leave the terrible-two phase behind. He'd only been with her an hour when she turned up the volume so loud that people kept looking over and wondering why he couldn't find the off switch.

"They better be true to their word about the kids club," he mumbled as he left his wife to rest. Right then, Mr Baskerville regretted asking Nancy along. Had she not been there he would have had the back up from Percy. Ada had clutched hold of his leg. He dragged her a step or two and then gave up and scooped her up and she laughed and started playing with his ears.

"Stop that. You're a big girl now," he said, a little concerned at how this family time was panning out. He watched his son and Nancy get out of the pool and then disappear down another beautiful staircase on their way to the games room. It wasn't that he didn't like Nancy or that he wasn't pleased for Percy to have someone his own age to hang out with but it was more that Ada was such hard work.

"Ah you've got your hands full there," smiled a couple of onlookers in the corridor. Mr Baskerville's heart sank further.

Chapter 16
Spain

The next day Mrs Baskerville was still unwell. Fortunately, true to its word, The Kids Club opened at nine and a nice young girl called Maria and someone in a giraffe costume took charge of young Ada. This left Mr Baskerville free to tend his wife and generally rest up before their hurricane of a three-year-old needed collecting.

His wife was propped up in bed now and half way through a thick novel. She barely spoke to him. It dawned on him that their relationship was on thin ice. How could this be? he asked himself, and when did it happen?

Sometime when they were **too** busy to notice he supposed. His wife turned a page. This holiday was meant to strengthen them as a family not to set them even further adrift, he thought gloomily. When had things got quite so bad?

The atmosphere merited that Mrs Baskerville put down her book for a short while to acknowledge her husband's presence. But she couldn't go as far as saying anything nice. She was so wearied by a number of things including Nancy's effervescence. "She's just so frothy," Mrs Baskerville complained. "There must be **something** wrong with her. Nobody gets handed a pack that good. And where does it come from? Her father's a no show and her mother…you've met her …inadequate."

"Harsh," said Mr Baskerville who liked Nancy's mother very much. "Fern is …"

"Fern's ditzy …at best. Nancy's sharp. You've heard her. She's well- informed…all that stuff about The Spanish wars of Succession. You name it she'll know about it. It's like she's swallowed Google. No one could say she was born with a silver spoon but…" Mrs Baskerville stopped for a moment and looked her husband in the eye before continuing, "It's like she thinks the world's her oyster. Watching little Nancy is like watching an Alchemist turning coal to gold."

As is widely known, holidays can put a test on friendship, as well as a marriage. After a couple of days, relationships in Room 66, too, were strained. In close quarters, Percy's halo dipped: shortcomings peeped through. Under scrutinization Nancy considered his capacity for fun and adventure were easily exhausted. Instead of peering ahead, alive to the kaleidoscope of possibilities, his was a wasteful gaze. His zestless approach spawned rampaging weeds in the garden of Nancy's mind. She felt threatened that these weeds might strangle her.

On this particular occasion she was riled that Percy dismissed without discussion her suggestion that they leave the hotel and explore. Nancy wondered if Mrs Baskerville was still ill or now just being fraudulent. It was upsetting the balance. The trips to see Flamenco dancing and the one out on a boat had both been cancelled.

 "Let's go and explore?" she asked again. *Their cover was safe so why wouldn't he abscond with her to explore downtown? The reward far outweighed the risk.*
"We have to stay in the hotel," said Percy.
"Mmm," said Nancy.
"Dad said," said Percy. "He said that he was sorry that they'd had to cancel the excursion."
"Worried about being found out…Cross parents? They never stay cross for long," she urged. "It's against their instinct. Unless of course you were Peter the Great or someone and Ed's not," she reasoned.

But Percy was unbudgeable. He argued it wouldn't be fair on his Dad. Nancy thought this was partially true but was more an excuse for being a massive-goody-two shoes.
"So, on this, there is no room for movement." she concluded.

Silence prevailed and briefly torn she found her *Screw You horn* had grown just a little bit taller. At this stage she went walkabouts and left Percy in the hotel room to stew in his own juice. It was unlikely he'd change his principled mind. He could be rigidly stubborn at times. She flounced down the marble stones and gave the two boys who'd displayed poor behaviour in the swimming pool a fiercesome look before heading for the hotel kitchen to gather supplies.

It was in this said kitchen that there began a series of events. Nancy was just on the verge of charming some edible provisions from one of the hard-pressed staff, when the chef, who Nancy recognised by his hat and disposition, started shouting in Spanish and weaponising utensils in a violent fit.

For a second, Nancy thought his ire was directed at her or the young woman that had just handed her some cheese and biscuits. Then Nancy saw a kerfuffle, and a kicking of the chef's legs and the emergence of a tri-coloured terrier screeching and tearing out of the kitchen followed by a long-legged waiter on its tail.

Enticed by this delightful, if beleaguered wiry-haired stray, Nancy joined the pantomime and she, too, took chase after this black, cream and toffee-coloured opportunist. The dog tore through the hotel as guests sipped their cool drinks deciding when they should take a dip in the elegantly mosaiced pool. It ran across the foyer, past the concierge and straight through the enormous wooden and glass door, which by chance had a new cohort of guests piling through with their rainbow of wheelies.

Like lightening, the dog shot out to the street on its short legs. Nancy, though nimbly in pursuit was stopped short by a porter who was blocking off the whole doorway with his bronze trolley. It was immediately followed by the slow entry of an elderly couple, one of whom had a very elaborate frame.

By the time Nancy was on the street the dog was nowhere in sight. She explored the vicinity and giving up on the dog took to exploration. She delighted in the narrow lanes full of bustle and stopped for ages to watch dogs at play in the dog park. An Appaloosa Poodle was on top of the climbing frame admiring the sea view and there was a furry little Pekinese in a peeked cap.
.

She made her way to the beach and was caught short by the beauty of the ocean, such a glorious coast line she couldn't remember ever seeing.

Blue lay on blue with the flatlining white fleck. Then, too, was the scent of the ocean. She noted the thin stemmed regal palm trees which thrilled her with their exoticism. In fact, the plant shapes, in general, were altogether amazing. One was Euphorbia Abyssinica her phone app informed her. Its nickname, Candelabra Spurge. She, then, switched off her phone.

Later, she claimed her phone had died. "Well I had too, really," she admitted to Percy when it had all calmed down.

Along this shoreline she walked barefoot on pale gold sand. She was feeling a pang of regret that Percy wasn't with her, when she saw two fishermen pulling their boat to shore.
She introduced herself and ascertained the one with just one front tooth was called Cloth.
What disappointed her was their reluctance to let her aboard and go back out to sea.
"Te puedo ayudar?" she said with gestures implying she might help with sorting the crabs or something.
"It's not as if you're diving for pearls," she said in English.
Apparently, they'd been out all morning and hardly caught a thing. The crabs weren't as plentiful as in the old days, they explained. Nothing but tourists. Nancy apologised for her status and then they sat down on the boat and exchanged cheeses and other goodies before the men packed up to go home.

Sandals in one hand, she walked on with the waves lapping at her feet before being overcome by the feeling that she should return to the hotel. But wouldn't hurry back and first she'd revisit the dog park. Then practise her Spanish along the stretch of tourist shops.

It was after a brief cambio-exchange with a certain shop keeper that the trouble began. Ill-advisedly, Nancy had explained to the woman at the Souvenir shop that she was in Spain without either mother or father and certainly wasn't on a school trip. The whole thing was maybe lost in translation or something because very shortly afterwards she was detained. She'd barely left the shop when she was stopped by the police and taken to a **booth** for processing.

Shamed and mortified, she felt little alternative than to spill the beans, dragging the Baskervilles into the messy affair. Consequently, The Baskervilles were summoned to hotel reception. Here they were met by two police officers. Mr Baskerville was required to return with one of them to the booth to identify and collect Nancy. Nancy and Mr Baskerville then returned to the hotel still under Civil Guard where the officers very publicly verbally stripped Mr and Mrs Baskerville off. Not even Ada could persuade them to go away until the right amount of flagellation had been metred out.

Sensibly, under the circumstances both Mr and Mrs Baskerville suitably prostrated themselves and earnestly explained in their clearest English, the depth of their negligence. They fully realized that they were *that* close to going to prison for child abuse. And Mrs Baskerville had had to doubly apologize for apparently looking as though she'd lost a button instead of a ten-year-old girl.

Afterwards, the policeman muttered that he hoped Mrs Baskerville recovered from her bug soon. The policewoman leant forward saying that she didn't want to be called out again. Mrs Baskerville tried not to recoil from the police woman's garlic breath.

As soon as the police were out the doors, Mrs Baskerville complained at the desk.
"Can I just say the Policia have treated me very badly," she said to the Concierge.
She then pulled Ada off to the lift and Nancy and Mr Baskerville followed, eyes down.
"He was only two generations from Franco," snarled Mrs Baskerville dismissively and decided she would be wise not to share her views with the Spanish.

Once back in the safety of their hotel room Mrs Baskerville continued to let out her indignity. "That Front-of-house chap glared at us quite unnecessarily," she said "He's lost a star. Anymore and I'm rating The Cervantes two star."

Mrs Baskerville once back in the comfort of the beautifully decorated room simmered down. She raised her head from her novel and observed, "That's another thing strange about Nancy. She seems to know everything and everyone. "*Nancy-Know-It -All*. That's what I'll call her."
"Shh. Not in front of Ada," said Mr Baskerville. He handed his wife a glass of red wine who, unused to Police brutality, drank it rather quickly. "I'm just not used to that level of aggression," she said. "Never been through such menacing. We should never have brought her."

Later the same day, Mrs Baskerville appeared with the family down by the pool. She was moved to see them all relaxed and laughing. Ada was perched on Nancy's lap being rocked back and forth to a song about ears hanging low. Ada was mesmerised.
"Everything alright Mrs Baskerville?" said Nancy.

"*Perfectly not,*" thought Mrs Baskerville before smiling back and saying, "Yes thank you Nancy." The words stretched out the corners of her lips producing a very wide smile that in no way married up with her eyes.

Nancy picked up Ada and plonked her on the chair beside her mother.

"Off for a swim," she declared.

"Anyone for tennis?" mouthed Mrs Baskerville sarcastically to her husband as soon as Percy had chased after the young girl in the turquoise bathing costume who performed a near perfect dive without an iota of aplomb.

"It's like Batman and Robin," continued Mrs Baskerville. "Don't ask me to have anyone else along on our family holiday ever again," she said and picked up an iced fizzy water wishing for a gin. "Ever!" she whispered emphatically slapping back down her glass with such force Mr Baskerville thought the stem might break. He thought the matter closed but only seconds passed before his wife confessed to him that she didn't have the patience for another of Nancy's capers.

Nancy (never one to shrink from a challenge) had left the group understanding that she wasn't going to win round Mrs Baskerville in a day.

Though before she left, on seeing Mrs Baskerville's glass going from half empty to empty, had instructed the barman to offer his assistance.

The barman excelled. Not only did he bring Mrs Baskerville a very generous gin and tonic but told her she should be banned from the hotel for being **too** good looking and making the other guests feel plain. Mrs Baskerville was clearly flattered.

Nancy had returned and offered to mind Ada for a while so the grown-ups could have some time in the pool. "I wonder if you care for a swim," she addressed Mrs Baskerville.
Mrs Baskerville declined.
"Have another lie down," Mr Baskerville said to his wife. "I'll do the children," he said swallowing "again" under his breath.

Chapter 17
Uno

Back in their hotel room Nancy said, "Your mum was livid. Anyone would think she'd been asked to saddle up for the Crimea. And through supper, I wish I could keep a po face for that length of time. How can you chew and still look so po? Did I tell you about the man I met with just a single tooth? An upper front. He was very chatty during the lunch we shared."
Nancy realized that it was an embellishment but what was a story without embroidery. Why restrict a colour range?

"She's not used to being in trouble…with, with anyone…let alone the Civil Guard," said Percy in defence of his mother.

Nancy changed the subject and talked about the Standard Poodles at The Dog Park, one with a lion-cut looking as if it had escaped from the ringmaster in a bygone age. And how delightful the Pekinese looked in its blue peaked cap.
This didn't even raise a smile from Percy who hadn't yet forgiven Nancy.
"Hardball is it?" thought Nancy and walked past

him.

That evening he laughed when Nancy described the unusually frosty look she'd received from Mr Baskerville when he'd gone to retrieve her.
"Would you say that Booth counts as prison. Have I been in the jail house, Percy?"
"Was it locked?" Percy asked.
Nancy didn't think so.
"I could see you in the legal profession…a regular Atticus Finch," said Nancy. "Though Atticus wasn't quite so squeaky clean by the time Harper Lee finished with him "Go Tell A Watchman."
Percy didn't know what she meant and didn't ask.

Back on the balcony of Room 66 they pulled up chairs and sat down to a game of cards.
"One for you, one for me…" he said

Once again, he felt her gaze. He stopped talking and instead fixated on dealing the cards.
When he looked up Nancy was still looking at him. He pursed his lips and blinked.
The two children were momentarily suspended in one of those pauses that really don't
happen very often. It was indeed a heavily pregnant pause.

"Numero Uno…please yourself first," said Nancy randomly or perhaps by way of an apology.
Percy looked at her and said, "Spoken like a true only child."
"Better than to build up hundreds and thousands of particles of tiny resentments," said Nancy. "Believe me, I don't say that we shouldn't give of ourselves, look out for others, of course we should. But loving thy neighbour as yourself? That's just not practical…nor is it to expect back what you put in. And I don't think Buddha was right either."
"Do you think Buddha's a good name for a dog?" asked Percy.
"Percy," she laughed.

At bedtime, they brushed their teeth together. Percy admired her teeth which were small, white and regular.

She had had to give the Baskervilles a solemn oath that she would not abscond again and even though they had extracted this promise Mr Baskerville kept knocking on the door and popping his head round to check they were OK.
"Just making a dummy with the pillows, Mr B" she teased him at bedtime.

When he'd gone she whacked Percy across the behind with one, as he was climbing into bed. He politely asked her not to take her frustration out on him.

"Ohhh," she said "They say familiarity breeds contempt."
Percy took his pillow and whammed her with it and a fight ensued, successfully emptying all pent-up emotion.
"Let me tell you a story," Nancy suggested as they got back into their beds. "About a swashbuckler, a regular dude and a dandy called Percy the Magnificent."
"May your stories get taller," said Percy sitting up.
"May you get taller and even more handsome," said Nancy and Percy blushed the colour of a summer rose.

By this time, he was leaning up on one elbow looking over at her. She could see his face in the dim light of their nightlamp.

She continued the story of the brave exploits of Percy the Magnificent and his face reminded her of a parrot feeding on ripe cherries. Maybe an orange-cheeked, bright-billed parrot found in the Peruvian jungle at a salt-lick amidst the blue and yellow and the scarlet of huge macaws.

The next day things had smoothed right over and as the days ticked by the family eased into a rhythm, some might go as far as to say harmony.

They swam and lazed by morning, went for walks around the town and built sandcastles on the beach in the afternoon. At night, they fine-dined and drank fancy drinks out of straws and rounded the evening off with cards.

Nancy delighted them with her shuffling. She'd whip the pack up, split the deck and had them march one by one practically into some sort of moving arc and back into two shuffled halves when she'd wham the first half back on the second before handing them back. And how she always seemed to win (especially if money was concerned) none of them could quite work out.

On one such evening, after a very satisfactory dinner, the Baskerville family plus Nancy sat on the terrace of room 67. They had a fine view of the pool. Ada had gone out like a light and the four of

them settled to a genial game of Uno with a pack borrowed by Nancy from a friend at reception. Mr Baskerville was playing diagonally across from Nancy. He couldn't remember ever coming across anyone quite so able to enjoy themselves.
"Don't you think she's a bit strange?" Mrs Baskerville asked her husband in a way he felt was refreshingly intimate. Although their holiday had got off to an incredibly bad start what with the plane delay, Ada screaming on and off, his wife projectile vomiting lobster bisque over the mirror in the bathroom and Nancy absconding and the ensuing indignity it provoked, it was now turning into a remarkably enjoyable occasion. His wife had recovered and was in an unusually mellow frame of mind. She was being pleasant and actually looking to him for support. He felt he *understood* Nancy but thought it wise not to admit it so he nodded his head.

"She's such a ..." usually very articulate Mrs Baskerville struggled to find the right adjectives. "bizarre little girl and **so** comfortable in her own skin. Most unnerving and I'd say plain unfair."
Mr Baskerville laughed.
"Makes the rest of us look as though we're on tamazapan," added Mrs Baskerville and narrowed

her eyes whilst Mr Baskerville opened his eyes and tilted his head to signify his engagement.

"Have you seen her whizz up and down that pool like an Olympian," continued Mrs Baskerville. "I was watching her from up here. Like an automaton she was. Perfect strokes, though she said she'd never even had a swimming lesson! She's had no after school classes in anything and yet speaks fluent French and her Spanish is better than ours. And she's learning Chinese."

Mr Baskerville remembered with fondness the year that they, not long married, had enrolled for evening Spanish classes.

"Sometimes we'd throw it and go for a drink instead," he reminded his wife.
"Well, we'd paid for a baby sitter," she said.
"I do like the way she and Percy bounce around together in the merriest of moods wafting good tidings to all. The hotel staff simply love them. Miguel is always running errands on their behalf. It was borderline appropriate when he bought Nancy that ice cream with three flavours, chocolate, vanilla, and tutti frutti. It must have cost him and he was clear that it hadn't been

misappropriated from the kitchen. She has the world at her feet."

His wife's mood continued to improve. Maybe recovery from intestinal issues had promoted joie di vivre or just a simple rest from the pressures of work, life or maybe it was partly due to the presence of this remarkable girl Nancy.
"She has the knack with Ada, too," said Mrs Baskerville.

Mr Baskerville remembered when he saw Nancy sitting in the Booth with her head hung low. She'd kept her eyes down throughout the walk of shame back to the hotel. But, the very second the officers had left the building this contriteness evaporated and Nancy burst into life, more buoyant than ever. She actually took Percy by the hand and ran off with him.

The way his son recounted Nancy's adventures left Mr Baskerville wanting to meet Cloth and picnic with the one-toothed sea-farer. It left him wanting to be the boy meeting Long John Silver and sharing a bite with hardened Spanish sea-farers.

"The deep blue sea Dad…" Percy told him, "One of them only had one tooth. Nancy said they shared their lunch with her. Olives as big as an egg she said."

Mr Baskerville listened and found it weirdly liberating. Nancy had a devil of an attitude. It made him realize how gingerly he walked through life, keeping to the shadows with one eye over his shoulder hoping he hadn't offended anyone.

"Dad, do you ever think that things just creep up on you?" said Percy.
"Wise beyond your years," said his father.
"She's got her game on Dad," said Percy.
"Yes, she's more on stage than backstage but not everyone's happy being centre of attention. Let's face it there's not room enough for everyone. Think Ada's got our share," he laughed patting his son on the shoulder.

Percy gave him a very fond smile and went to his room.
"Yes," he said to his wife who was now reading her book.
"There's something strange about Nancy."

All in all, they had to agree it had been a very good day.

Mrs Baskerville seemed most alive when the focus was Politics and hearing from Percy her qualities and how committed to her work she was Nancy ascertained she'd be good in government. "Ever thought of running to be a MP? I think you'd make a good one," Nancy asked her one meal time.
Mrs Baskerville took it as an enormous compliment and couldn't remember anyone articulating such faith in her and so earnestly.

A bird's eye view of the Baskerville family plus one around a table laughing together; sipping drinks by the pool could judge them favourably on the blessed stakes.

Though on the last evening but one, Nancy seeing the Baskerville's so happy and at ease, felt a violent missing of Fern. She grabbed the stairwell rails in a sort of panic she climbed the steps, each bringing her nearer to privacy and to mum rehab.

Adeptly, she managed the key, grabbed her phone and flung herself on the bed and phoned home.

Thoughts of Fern swam round her head. Fern curled up on the old sofa with the saffron walls of their den decked in mildly hippy Namastes and pictures of dogs for Nancy.

Saffron was her mother's favourite colour and now Nancy thought it a beautiful colour too. Anticipating a long call, Nancy snuggled down on the bed. Her stomach fell when Fern didn't pick up straight away then she heard her mother's cheerful voice and imagined her face. The kitchen clock above the white kitchen cabinets showed the one hour time difference. There was a lone apple in the fruit bowl: her artwork on the walls. All was well.

**Chapter 18
Homewards**

The next morning, they left the hotel in good spirits and had no delays or mishaps before boarding their flight. Nancy proudly wheeled along her smart turquoise cabin bag as if it were a pet dog on a lead.

Once the plane had taken off she peered out of the window watching the Spanish infrastructure shrink and miles of sea stretch out below them. When the view was entirely obscured by clumps of cumulous clouds Nancy rose from her seat, and maneuvered herself past Percy into the aisle. Everyone presumed she was going to the loo. However, she went off in the opposite direction.

Why let a harassed face or two get in the way of having a good investigation into the flight deck?
"But I want to know if a plane has a hand break," she said, slipping past the blonde air hostess in trousers into the cockpit so that she was literally looking over the captain's shoulder.
"You can't be in here," said an alarmed co-pilot. Nancy felt time was of the essence as they'd only get procedural.

"Is it not safe?" asked Nancy turning her back on the co-pilot and speaking directly to the pilot.
"He's right you know. Better get back to your parents," said the pilot.
Nancy admired the impressive amount of gadgetry on the cockpit.
"Yes." agreed Nancy. "Is it true a plane can fly itself? Not saying that pilots aren't highly skilled with hours and hours and hours of flying experience. If an individual is able to write formulae that most teachers can't seem to follow…."
The pilot laughed.
"Ask Issy to give you details of pilot training. She's the one with the trousers. Now get…"

As Nancy walked back up the aisle she noticed Mr Baskerville's stricken face and smiled assuringly at him. Mrs Baskerville, who wore a thick quilted eye-mask and had a podcast on, (timed for about the length of the flight), hadn't noticed Nancy's escapade and was oblivious to the whole incident. Percy was open-jawed. "Well it was so tempting," said Nancy sitting back down in her seat and buckled up.

"I've hardly been in a plane and I wanted to see

how they worked. They're incredible. This Boeing 737 is an amazing piece of technology. If Orvil and Wilbur could only know how far their wing exploration had come. I must check out the Boeing 787…a bigger aircraft all together I'd imagine," she said.
She relaxed back into her seat with an air of contentment.

Next thing, an air steward handed her some paper with links on from the captain and a little note attached saying, *The sky's the limit.* Nancy beamed and Percy's jaw dropped again.
"Maybe I'll be a pilot, too," he said.

They soared home over the channel undisturbed by any doodlebug.

Once home on English soil they drove straight to Langton Green. A thin mist of cloud seemed to follow them the entire journey. Nancy was dropped off first.

"A partial success?" Mr Baskerville suggested to his wife who'd retained the right to remain silent. Fern noticed Mrs Baskerville had stayed in the car when dropping Nancy off. If it hadn't been for

Mrs Baskerville's face Fern might have been able to put it down to her enthusiasm to get home but instinct informed her that Nancy had led them a bit of a dance.

Nancy braced herself for maternal ire. However, Fern had some explaining of her own to do. In the short week that Nancy had been away a lot had happened at Number 23 Lavender Gardens. A boyfriend had appeared fresh out of Tinder and moved in. His name was Gareth.

"Life's not always what you expect it to be," sighed Fern as she placed a bowl of tomato soup and two triangles of buttered bread down before Nancy.
"We just clicked," she smiled at her daughter.
"Jeeze mum I was only gone a week," said Nancy scraping her chair nearer the table while attempting to dispel the unwelcomed idiom *Be careful what you wish for*.

Nancy thought back to March when the snow was cold on the ground and Fern had seemed so drained of life.

"This is good news," she told her mother whilst picturing a wrecking ball in her head smashing through their saffron snug. "But isn't moving in a little soon?"
"When you know you know. It's a grownup thing," smiled Fern.

Nancy felt her mother was not really grown up but kept quiet. Fern deserved a break. Maybe this time it would be different. Besides it **might** mean a dog or a sibling.
"Does he work from home?" Nancy asked.

A dog would make them a four. Mum would have whatever his name was and she would have an African Hunting Dog cross Dingo-Spaniel or the nearest match. She dipped her buttered triangles into her soup. The triangles reminded her of the large ears of her ideal dog she so ardently wanted.

"I'll need a decent computer with you two all…hand in hand …. on the sofa. I hope he's minted," Perhaps she could get a pony too? *Keep your powder dry girl, about the dog.* She'd ask him first.
"Comfortable," said Fern. "His wife's in their house. Gareth has teenagers… Jack and Milly. Go

to school in Leamington," continued Fern deciding to get it all out in the open.

Nancy felt the baby thing was looking less likely but the dog question was a real runner. Gareth would be on the back foot, as would Fern for bringing a stranger into their home and on such short notice. A big dog was now not out of the question.

Gareth **did** add something to the household that very weekend. He bought Fern a *sit up and beg* bike, complete with a basket. They all went out for a ride that Sunday. It had been quite strenuous so they were delighted to see an Ice cream van parked, on the village green, between the willows. "Simple pleasures," Gareth remarked and did all the queuing and paying. Fern nodded in agreement.

Fern and Nancy lay their bikes on the grass, and sat under the shade of a tree.
There, gazing at the brook, the three of them sat in a row holding their golden cones and licked ice creams: one pink, one green, one brown. It all seemed very civilized in a nice fuzzy way. Fern had a definite bloom. Nancy realized she alone

wasn't enough for her mother anymore. She felt Gareth just had to be a dog lover and watched out for signs. He could be the catalyst in the magic dog producing formula because in Nancy's head it was all about ingredients, in one shape or another. Nancy had once heard someone say that if you got on the wrong train then all the stations were wrong. She very much hoped Gareth was the right train and that the next stop would involve four legs and a wagging tail.

Chapter 19
Peanut butter and Jam

After school, Percy was waiting for Nancy at their usual spot. She found him reading a Who Dunnit on the corner.
"The clues are there," he said. "Just have to work it out. Agatha worked at a chemist… knew about poison," said Percy returning *Murder is Easy* to his bag.
"Think you'd make a good detective…razor sharp," remarked Nancy.

Being with Nancy was like that. A few put downs then a compliment that would have you smiling the whole week.

First off, they picked up provisions from Nancy's before heading over to Percy's. Nancy with the jar of peanut butter and the damson jam safely in her bag, was swinging the pack of sliced white bread backwards and forwards in an easy motion. But as they rounded the corner to Jasmine Crescent, Percy asked her to put it in her bag.
"The neighbours might see," he said.
He looked so worried Nancy stashed it without further ado.

Together they made a generous stack of sandwiches and took them out on to the verandah with a carton of juice.

The two children delighted in squishing the malleable white bread into the delicious blend of peanut butter and jam. Percy stared at the deep purple, white, yellow and tan combination and further squidged at the bread before burying his teeth into the battered triangles.

"You are such an animal," said Nancy pouring apple juice. "I think you'd be a lion in the animal kingdom. Or maybe a lemur," she giggled. "Mmm this damson jam is gorgeous. It's a miracle mum chose it over the wine in the Tombola."

"My mum's limiting juice now. It's water, water, water, everywhere," said Percy who had slightly coloured over the lion remark. "Filtered, of course."

"Mrs Baskerville is into all things nutritional. You'll probably live to 125. I bet your dad's having a Mars Bar on the QT or a KFC," said Nancy.

"Mum says the brain and the body are not separate. She'd throw one if she saw us doing this," and he took a wide bite from the sandwich.

Nancy looked at him with affection and raising her chin with her eyes still fixed on him, slowly drank her apple juice.

"We're all hormones Percy. It's a counter system. But **next time** we'll get Fanta," she said. "We're young and metabolically healthy enough to mop up the blood sugar. We'll pack it up at fifteen." They laughed and then Nancy leaned forward. "Show us your muscles Percy."

Percy put his sandwich down and flexed his forearm attempting a manly stance.

"Yes, that's enough muscle to soak up the sugar in a peanut sandwich. You've enough tissue to act as a reservoir to get it out of the bloodstream. I think it's to do with insulin and its sensitivity… if it can take up Insulin it can take up the sugar. That's what we're eating here, sugar and salt," she laughed.

"So, what's Insulin?" said Percy

"A Hormone," said Nancy.

"Oh, I've heard about those. They call it Peanut butter and **jelly** in America," said Percy.

"Yes-jelly," said Nancy pulling a face that brought laughter into her aqua-marine eyes and a wide smile showing her perfect white teeth.

"Has Ada ever had a Mars bar?" asked Nancy.

"I don't think so," spluttered Percy and shook his head.

"Packet of crisps?" suggested Nancy and slapped her thighs raising her carton and smashed it against Percy's, precipitating a slight howl.

"I think I'm in heaven," said Nancy. "Waste not want not," and snatched the last sandwich. She licked her lips in feigned ecstasy, relishing the look on Percy's face as he stared at the diminishing triangle.

"Here you are," she said and handed him the sandwich with a perfect crescent bite out of it which he took willingly and chewed it lovingly.

"You know that I never heard your mum or dad say the "No" word to Ada throughout the whole holiday."

"Yes they do, in some respects, excel in Modern parenting," said Percy.

"We did have a good time, didn't we? I loved the Hotel Cervantes," said Nancy. "Shall we sing to the birds?"

"Seems only fair…though they might prefer the bread," said Percy.

"How about the nation's favourite song? You'll recognize it. Mum used to play it all the time, in her Elton John phase."

They stood up and faced the garden fence. The blackbird flew back and forth.
"It's a little bit funny," Nancy sang.
Percy who could hold a tune, too, joined in at,
"This feeling inside."

They sang the first verse together and then Percy sat down. Nancy who knew all the words carried on. Percy thought her singing very lovely.
"In the old days people sang a lot more I think. Good for the breathing my mother's Yoga teacher told us. She had to take me along. We used to go everywhere together," said Nancy sitting back down next to Percy.

Seeking further amusement, Nancy asked if they could explore the garage.
"Nobody uses them for cars anymore," said Percy as he masterfully pressed the gadget that electrically opened the door, revealing the Baskervilles secrets.
Nancy glanced around as she entered.
"This would make an excellent club house," she declared. "You're so lucky having all this space,"
"Mum said our house is a rabbit hutch and doesn't like it at all," said Percy.

"But your garden's great. It has **two** cherry trees. And you've got four bedrooms. All big," said Nancy.

"Mum says you can't swing a cat in two of them. She makes Dad sleep in the spare room half the time so we do need four really. It was meant to be a guest room but we never have guests," said Percy.

Nancy had heard enough. "Look at the toboggans! We are going to have **so** much fun this winter. I'm sure Gareth will take us to Edge Hill. He likes fishing you know. I bet he catches them **this** big," she said in a funny voice, stretching her arms wide, bursting into laughter, making Percy join in. "This big," he mimicked and Nancy shook her head enthusiastically.

"We'll be bombing down the slopes come winter," said Nancy assuredly.

Percy kept quiet as he didn't like winter and wasn't crazy about snow either, especially when it lost its crispy whiteness and hardened up to ice. Once, he'd slipped and hit his head so hard he needed A and E. His mother, by his side, had stressed so hard about missed work meetings.

He'd actually heard her asking why the school hadn't rung his dad. Nancy continued to rootle. "Anyone for tennis? It's so heavy, whose was it? Great Uncle Lancelot's?" she said waving a wooden tennis racket with gusto and then quickly putting it back, as she caught sight of a badminton set complete with net. She had it set out on the lawn in a flash.

When Mr Baskerville returned with Ada, he joined in. Ada was officially made ball girl, the most important job of the game and Nancy promised to give her lessons in *BadMINGtom* as soon as she was four.

"Bad Ming tom!" Ada mouthed back to Nancy who was crouching down at eye level with her. She and Ada clapped their hands with delight. When Mrs Baskerville arrived home the tournament was still going on and even she had a brief go before excusing herself *as someone had to cook supper*.

When they came in from the garden in the radiance of a post exercise high, with Ada trailing behind, quiet as a lamb, looking up adoringly at Nancy, Mrs Baskerville couldn't stop herself from commenting, "I don't know where you get your energy?"

"Through my mitochondria, I believe," replied Nancy.

Mr and Mrs Baskerville just looked at her.

Nancy's eyes were dead pan. Then they darted from side to side and an infectious laughter peeled out from her mouth. Ada, who like others, had no idea what she was laughing at, joined in. Mrs Baskerville's shoulders dropped and as she ran the cold tap to fill a saucepan, she felt quietly relaxed. She even asked Nancy if she would like to stay for supper.

It was on the way home from this cordial occasion that Nancy saw Kevin the Labradoodle and a vision came to her.

Images of the toboggans she'd seen at Percy's garage conflated with Kevin and the idea of some sort of dog cart was born. Put wheels on the toboggan, thought Nancy, and they needn't wait until snow. A dog-cart.

On the short passage home Nancy's fancies grew, unfurling carts pulled by three or four or even five of the neighbourhood dogs. Percy in one and she in the other. They could race. If they went to school in them she wondered if the caretaker could take the dogs back home after their school-run or **even** set up a makeshift doggy day-care in the school grounds. Nancy realized that this might seem highly impractical but wouldn't it make sense if you could drop your child off and your dog off on the way to work? It would breach some rule and her mother's words rang out in her head. *You need permission to sneeze these days.*

She was sure Gareth would help her as men like him usually did. He'd be good at that sort of thing; besides his tools were using up half the shed. "You're handy with a spanner," she'd say to Gareth and they'd bond nicely building a couple of carts.

Before doing anything else, once back at Lavender Gardens, she dragged out her yellow canvas chair and put it squarely under the apple tree. She unfolded a notebook Fern had given her with the motto *You can do anything* (which she wholly disagreed with) took out a ruler, protractor and a couple of sharp pencils, and with the help of You Tube, set to work on her design. She prettified the background with the coloured pencils you dip in water, bought with the intention to decorate her bedroom with a canine display. The Art teacher at her last school had told Fern that she had prestigious talent and if she chose Nancy could copy anything. She decided not to draw in any dogs on the go-cart design. *Gently Gently.*

When she was happy with her design she put it away and leaned back in her chair.

The unmistaken melody of a blackbird pierced the garden with song. When would they know more about the language of birds? Once she had asked Miss McBride when she'd been on playground duty, if she thought a robin could understand a blackbird?

"Or a Magpie understand other members of the Corvine family?" Miss McBride had replied.

"All they ever bang on about **is** the mating," said Nancy. Miss McBride had nodded her head in agreement but she seemed a little sad.

Chapter 20
School

Tuesday morning, on their way to school, Nancy pulled out her go-cart design and showed Percy who was so impressed he stopped in his tracks.

"Going to build it with Gareth, one for you and one for me, and we don't need the toboggans. Gareth can get wood," Nancy explained.
"Brakes, and everything Nancy," Percy said patting her on the back. "I can't wait to see it on the…**go**." This wasn't quite true.

On arrival at school Nancy received a complete surprise. Her classmate Amrita asked to nominate her for Form Leader.

Nancy heard herself say, *Yes*. In the back of her mind, she thought, in some way, it might help her mission to get a dog by indicating that she was super responsible. At the very least, it would be a distraction from the slow burn of desire.
"Did you ask me so that I could suggest you?" Nancy asked.

"Oh no," said Amrita with a vehement shake of the head. "Just think you'd be good."
Amrita gave her a collegiate smack on the back which both warmed and worried. Nancy, who wasn't one to go back on her word was already beginning to regret that she'd agreed to the nomination.

All day Nancy looked at her classmates with fresh eyes.
"This is a formidable task … a skin thickening operation," she said to Amrita who assured her of Pash's and Amelia's vote.
"At least Fleur…super-popular, can't run cos she's already been Form Leader," said Amrita.
"Wonder who I'll be up against?" said Nancy.

Two boys were nominated to run alongside Nancy. Josh was the class football star. Charlie, that perfectly nice, all-rounder. It was to be a three-horse race.

Throughout the day Nancy laid on thick compliments to all swing voters.
"It reminds me of Van Gogh. I saw it at the Louvre when we lived in France," she said to Jack about his painting. He was chuffed.

At lunch, she talked to who she could including Claire, a very complex child. Claire asked if Nancy would come to play at hers at the weekend. Nancy used the *maybe* word and profoundly felt the ageing effects of politics. She sacrificed a really good pencil to escape further involvement. But it did spell out the true-sense of the word *maybe* which was in itself galvanising. *What did it matter if she won the whole school round if she didn't have a dog?*

That afternoon Nancy and Amrita watched eagle-eyed as Miss McBride explained there would be hustings where each candidate would have a spot each to explain why they would make a good form leader and be the best choice.

Nancy thought Miss McBride was rolling it out a little heavy.
"Res-pon-sib-ility." It was all growly Rs and hissing s's, brutal b's and tutting "t"s.
Miss McBride missed the bell and this meant Year 5 was last out of the school-gates. Usually, she was the best teacher in the school at time management. That afternoon Percy had had to wait ten minutes at *their* corner which he did so very patiently.

More often than not it was the other way around and it was Nancy waiting for him. She'd be in some feline pose doing her homework.

Today, before they'd even said *hello* Nancy threw up her hands at him, nearly poking his eye out.
"Look! The vote's tomorrow," she said. "Are you going to help me?"
Percy hadn't seen her like this and thought her tone snippy.
"Could you offer them something?" he suggested.
"Obviously!" she retorted charging down the street without so much as a hint of apology for her poor time-keeping.
"I've got a speech to write," she threw back at him.
"They never did anything like that when I was in Year 5," he said.
"Times change," said Nancy.
"I don't know what you expect me to do," said Percy a little helplessly.
"Well, for starters you can ask Will to tell his brother to vote for me."
Percy didn't reply.
"Well lucky I don't mind losing then," laughed Nancy thinking how she could mix it up a little on the way down.

"Not like I'll be dropped in hot oil if I lose or put in a knife-filled barrel or have my head shaved or put on stage with my head down and arms tightly bound behind my back and have children invited to spit at me," said Nancy with her mood lightening, probably in some way down to her powerwalk along Lavender Way.
"It's the taking part that matters…" Percy laughed.

As she started the *one two, one two* on the road home with a bag slung over her shoulder her mind shimmied with ideas. Percy felt her very distracted. She was walking so quickly he just let her get on with it. She was taking bigger and bigger strides, knowing she couldn't rest until happy with her proposal. Word perfect. Delivered with confidence. Nice and slow.

On galloped Nancy's thoughts as she turned the last corner home. There, she waited for Percy to catch up.

"Outdoor classes, Mango Tango, bring a pet to school, bring a dog to school, Swap a-treat Wednesdays, No-school Thursdays," she bombarded him with her latest suggestions. "That

Charlie Wilson...he's got Head Boy written all over him let alone Form Leader."

"Through him like Brighton Rock," agreed Percy. "It's like running against a Kennedy. What we need to discover is his Chappasomething."

"No time. I won't go down and dirty on him. I'll just go through him," assured Nancy with her lips in a perfect heart-shape and her head giving just a hint of a nod.

"How about Matinee Monthly or Film Friday Fortnight," said Percy.

"I like that one," said Nancy.

They slapped each other on the hands.

To stand a chance, Nancy knew she would need to be radical...to create a need.

"Are we victims of coercive control...heads down, sat at our tables deprived of Vitamin D," suggested Nancy.

"That would make Miss McBride out as a prison guard. I thought you liked her?" said Percy feeling *being radical* wasn't for him.

"Could I promise Logan that he could be head of the football team?" suggested Nancy.

"Undemocratic and not in your remit. Hope you're not developing a goddess complex, Nance. It's Langton Primary not North Korea,"

With furled eyebrows, Nancy poked him half intimating she was practising for that all important button.

"How about we ask the state to pay children to go to school?" said Nancy taking herself seriously and thrilled by her new angle. "Up front. In their pockets… for their participation? Their money would grow the economy as well as anyone else's"

"Pocket money for pupils. Has a definite ring. But it's a little too grass roots for our objective. You're only going for Form Leader. It's only for a term," Percy reminded Nancy. He was wondering what there would be to eat at his house and that no doubt Nancy's biscuit tin would be at least half-full.

"Well it is on us school kids in'it… the great oligarchic system, controller of Capitalist democracies and wealth distribution rely on," said Nancy and sang a bar or two of a song *"No pupil, no dime."*

"You've lost me Nance," said Percy.

"Got any dirt on the opposition?" Nancy asked.

"That Charlie is as stiff as un umbrella. Think I'll say that to him in front of the class. Or, I've heard you don't capture your emissions Jack? Suggest he wears a nappy?"

Percy burst out laughing and spluttered, "That's a bit below the belt."

"Literally! Well they say politics is messy."

"Aren't you meant to let them *go low* so you can *go high*?" said Percy.

"No seriously," she slowed and caught Percy's sleeve. "My only real chance and the straightest line to a block vote would have been to win Fleur and her friends but I've hardly spoken to them since I started Langdon.

.

Before they said goodbye Nancy told Percy, "My proposal will be no longer than two and half minutes or the length of one A4."

"So, game on for tomorrow?" asked Percy.

"Is the sun still planning to rise?" Nancy replied. They parted as was their habit ever since Percy had been allowed to walk home alone on the corner of Lavender Gardens and Jasmine Crescent.

Before entering the house, Nancy sat down in the back garden, chewing over thoughts with barely half an eye on her surroundings. Ideas swam like fishes through her mind, springing images, spawning baby ideas. The whole venture was awash with possibilities. These ideas began to throw off finished conclusions…she imagined dog

Friday a reality. A dalmatian comes to visit and everyone is tantalized as she explains its Croatian roots and about the sixpence used by Crufts to measure the spots.

At present, it was just a whirl of untameable ideas, pecking as incessantly as a woodpecker at a tree. Once inside the house, after grabbing a glass of milk, a packet of fig rolls and a banana, Nancy locked herself in her bedroom and googled the Gettysburg Address.
Then she googled Public speaking. Drill down seemed to be the soundbite of the moment but she wouldn't use it as it sounded like an allusion to fossil fuel, the current enemy to humanity.

Her fingers started flying over her keyboard hitting the delete key again and again as she struck off unnecessary words with ruthless precision. She, too, would amaze by brevity. She added a little Chairman Mao and Martin Luther King's, *Free, free, free at last* but couldn't find a match with The Declaration of Independence.

She started by not promising the undeliverable but soon decided that that wouldn't get votes.

Better to promise whatever they wanted but what was that? There was no alternative but to give it the *Go Bold or Go Home* treatment. Tell them what they wanted. *But should she evangelize?*

With no ink in the family printer she had to write it out by hand, and then ventured out of the bedroom for the first time that evening to practise it in front of the landing mirror.
"If you ain't searchin. You're lost." *Cheesy was good in politics,* Nancy felt. *Aim for sweet spot between modern and too American, before the rub.*
"If we're content with the status quo, we're not growing," she said to the mirror but it said nothing back. *Was she happy with the "we" thing?*
"Don't we hold our own keys?" she said and shook her hand as if holding a bunch of them, thinking that would be her new mantra.
"Pupils hold up 90 per cent of the sky. She would begin with. **More** trips, **more** outside learning, a class pet, **more** dancing, rowing and swimming." She'd thought long and hard about the dancing and decided to stick with it.

She'd whizzed hurriedly round the class girls on a quick fact-finding mission.

"Gliding lessons…surely essential," she practised saying it out loud. She would be radical. They would say, "That was a tour de Force"
Should she finish with a joke in a deep voice: *Here endeth the first lesson* or would that be in poor taste? *This PC world of competing sensitivities was a mine-field of do's and don'ts.*
Fern called Nancy for supper. She might have told her about the leadership competition over the familiar sight of fishfingers, yellow and fresh new potatoes and large, green peas; but decided against it with Gareth there.

During supper she was distracted thinking how best to appeal. She thought she might tell a brief war story about Bounce the sea-faring dog of Napoleon that came to a sticky end. Ideas continued to brew and mix with others fermenting and bubbling all through the meal like Lord Nelson's intestinal issues. During a dessert of peaches and Cornish ice cream (the new delight Gareth had introduced to their household) she had an idea to concoct a new type of fighting competition that included biting, pinching and scratching. Though almost instantaneously she knew that dog wouldn't hunt.

Maybe, she thought as she scooped a peach, she should just promise the impossible.
Close the school on Wednesdays. The French did it and if she just dropped her standards of veracity she could promise anything. Peaches with cream and ice-cream. *Chips **and** rice.*

Fern excused Nancy from any washing up on account of her project.

What they must realize is that I am the jewel in their crown. I'll have to plug the dance card to woo the triple alliance?" Nancy e-mailed Percy.
"The Triple Alliance?" Percy felt himself emerged in something he didn't quite get.
"Lily, Abigail and Maya," typed Nancy. "The Influencers."
"Oh them," answered Percy.
"Going to learn whether I'm good under fire?" she wrote.
"You'll be fine," emailed back Percy thinking what else could he say.

Her speech finished, as her head hit the pillow Nancy wondered how she would sleep. She forced out images of potential voters, replaced her classmates with a train of cockerpoos.

But when she saw the dim light of the next morning she was once again met by an emotional jungle. She rose, washed and dressed and imagined that her Yellow friend, a medium to big-sized dog with generously large and beautifully pointed ears, was in her garden waiting, in a perfect humour, to go on their pre-school morning run.

Dragged back to the real world, she toyed with an argument for more uniform-free days.
"A MUFTI day is a chance to define yourself. A chance to stand out and not just blend into a sea of collective green," she mouthed semi out loud as she went downstairs to breakfast.

Meeting Percy on the corner, he felt Nancy looked rather worn.
"It's a tough road but you don't have to walk it alone," he said and listened as Nancy practised her speech on him.
"If I take one far below the belt Percy you'd hope it will make me stronger."
"Go for that power vacuum Nance…suck them in," and he put his lips together in a sucking motif and Nancy burst out laughing and then joined in.

"I shall fill them with the light of day," said Nancy.

"Get on up," said Percy. "Dance crazies?"

"Check," she said.

"Party lovers and dresser-upers?"

"Check," she said.

"Animal lovers?"

"Check," she said

"Got to offer food!" Percy suggested "Pizzas maybe."

"How about meals at the Happy Panda," said Nancy.

"My great, great aunt told me they once found orange fur in a fridge inspection. It was in the Oxford Herald," said Percy.

"Would blend well with sweet and sour sauce," said Nancy. "Cat...do you think?"

"My aunt said cats and dogs...more specifically Alsatian fur," said Percy.

"Well that's not a nice thought," said Nancy. "How did they…"

She didn't continue. They were at the school gates.

"Good luck," said Percy.

"Thanks Alistair Campbell," said Nancy.

Percy looked puzzled but gave her the thumbs up and an open grin.

Chapter 21
The Vote

What on earth am I doing? Nancy questioned herself on the day of the vote. She knew she'd have to concentrate hard to get through it.

With a dry throat, Nancy sat through the register. "It's time for our three candidates to explain to us why they would make the best Form Leader." announced Miss McBride who had adopted a natty royal blue trouser suit for the occasion. "Normally we would call them in alphabetical order, but not today," she continued as she placed three names in a Beanie hat and beckoned Amrita to pick out the first.

Nancy sat still and watched Josh Harvey move to the front of the class. Amrita stood by with a large glass egg timer.
"Just to remind Class 5 before Josh speaks. We will limit the talk to three minutes. The ballot will be SECRET," said Miss McBride. "I won't be asking you to vote by putting your hands up. This time you'll get a piece of paper with three names on it. Put a cross by your choice. It must be legible to count. Remember you are not voting for your

friend but the person best equipped to lead us to the end of term."

Josh was shifting his stance from side to side and when given the nod he was like a greyhound fresh out of the starting gate. Luckily you got the general gist quite easily: Football, football, football. He said, "Football should be played all year round."

He promised a new super team, more away matches and further afield. Countrywide. Trips to watch the games, too. These would be open to girls. He advocated they ought to have more space on the walls to hang photographs of top scorers. He further crooned on about the beautiful game advocating there should be a school anthem for the players. He wasn't short of ideas. It was if he was a senator in an expanding Roman Republic. He talked of football trips and a tournament and how glorious it would be to be in the winning team. He wanted the entrance hall to be a display for Football Valour, with a Hall of Fame.

Nancy felt it hard to constrain her excitement. *He was shooting himself in the foot surely? Over and over again. Talk about own goals.* Then when Miss

McBride rang a little bell, he stopped mid-stream, crumpled the piece of paper up and kicked it into the audience who fell about with laughter. It was hard not to be impressed by such compelling swagger. Nancy, **now,** saw to what extent he was pushing through a well-oiled door.

She was next to speak and it was a hard act to follow. She walked up to the front of the class and had to wait for Josh's applause to stop before she started. He was sat casually at his desk grinning from ear to ear.

She delivered her two-minute proposal well. "The Beautiful Game," she sighed and looking straight out at the audience she agreed that all sport and outside engagement were important. She looked at her sheet of A4.

"Ninety per cent of the school is its pupils. We hold up the sky. Each and **every** one of us matters. You are ALL important. Change doesn't happen by itself. It is MADE. Without it we don't grow." She stamped her foot. "Here are my sug-gestions," she pronounced with a hard and then a soft "g."

One.   More away from classroom-based learning…Fresh air is fun. New sights inspire.
Two   Dress up Friday Fortnight…self-expression is important.
Three   Ban all tests for the first two terms.
Four   Allow a Class Pet preferably a dog.
Five   Year 5 and 6 End of year School Dance.
Six   Weekly trips…somewhere in groups.
Seven   Every Monday morning start with a film.

The tables looked bigger, the faces a little strange. All Nancy could hear was the scrapping of chairs as she returned to her seat to lukewarm applause. Never had she wished so hard for home time. She could hardly concentrate through Charlie's proposal but could tell it was polished. For one thing, Amrita was giving her looks all the way through it, as if to say, *Well, that's his dad talking or his mum wrote that.*

"Now the candidates have given us their proposals. Will they come up to the front?" said Miss McBride.

Charlie White looked sideways at her. He was central. An advantage but at least she was on his right. Long ago she'd noted by watching TV presenters when the format was two of them the one the eye went to most was on the right. Josh looked the most relaxed.

The class applauded them. Lucas Green shouted out, "Vote Josh!" in a very loud voice.
To do her justice Miss McBride gave him such a hard stare back that he desisted but not before he'd muttered, "keep your wig on," loud enough to provoke tittering.
"Sit back down candidates," said Miss McBride. "Give out the voting slips Lily," she continued and produced a package of tiny pencils.
"You been to the bookies Miss?" said Lucas again and started laughing…turning around in his chair and giving pretend header gestures.
Nancy saw Amrita throw her eyes up.
"Lucas, only those present will get their votes counted," said Miss McBride firmly.

She was glistening with pride as she announced it was the first time, to her knowledge, that the school had held a secret ballot.

Nancy's mind flashed momentarily back to a discussion she had once had with Miss McBride concerning the travesty of the US voting system.

Nancy bore down on her sense of preservation and remembered the usefulness of her mother's creed. *It's just fate, Nancy.*

She shook herself mentally. She felt it was a foregone conclusion and mourned that time spent and passion burnt.

Miss McBride asked Aiden and Abigail to collect, then count the votes. Abigail beamed at this opportunity. Aiden shuffled after wiping away his lengthy fringe from his eyes every few seconds. It was clear that the piles were uneven. Amrita turned to look at Nancy who was motionless in her chair.

It didn't go her way. The scores were written on the whiteboard under the title Leadership Contest. The number **five** stood out to Nancy like a crucifixion in the desert sands. It so overpowered her rods and cones that her ears rang. So, this was what it was like to want to disappear she thought. LAST! She'd come Last! Nailed her colours to the mast and come last.
Josh, ten. Charlie, twelve. Nancy, five.

She had lost and by a huge margin. It was horrible. Anger and a sense of disbelief coursed through her. *How could everyone be so short-sighted? Surely her suggestions would have been far more fun and productive?*
Open air study, out of school learning, extra art and drama, film Friday alternated with dress down and dress up Friday: favourite of all, class pet.
Oh, fading dreams.

"There can only be one winner," Charlie said as he brushed by her at break time.
But why? she'd thought. *Round tables, coalitions, joint leaderships…*
"Well done you," she said and hoped he'd float into space on his ego.
She could kick herself for agreeing to take part.
What had she been thinking?

By home time Nancy was quite relieved not to have won as Charlie had to stay behind and discuss parents' evening with Miss McBride. This minimized the disappointment though the shame was going to be tougher to shift. She was glad she hadn't told her mum about the sorry affair.

"Five," said Percy "That's more than I'd have got against those two. And you're new."
"So much for the New Broom theory," said Nancy.
"Mm…well you've only lost something you didn't want that much," said Percy.
"I've lost far more now. My …my dignity," said Nancy.
"That's not true," said Percy.
"I thought I'd be in for a chance with those ideas," said Nancy.
"Maybe they're just not ready for…" said Percy.
"Well if they want virtually no change whatsoever…" said Nancy.
"Transitions take patience. Look you've cut your teeth," said Percy.

Nancy felt like biting someone but said nothing.
"Try again next term. Look if you can…," said Percy.

"Oh Percy …get real…I'm done with it." With that she stomped her foot as if the whole affair was on the pavement but tagging alongside inside her was a humbling defeat not a resounding victory: an unwelcome guest.
"And don't tell Ed," she shouted over her shoulder.

When Percy video-called her later she said she was sorting her Chakras. Percy thought the influence might have sprung from Fern and considered he hadn't really a clue what his mum or dad believed in.

"I will not be reduced. Next year I'll be Form Leader and Head Girl," said Nancy.

Percy thought her eyes exquisite.

"But they don't have a Head Girl or Boy at our school."

"They will do next year," said Nancy. "Percy. We are one thing and another."

When she rang off these words floated in the air. He liked the saying *I will not be reduced* and had heard somewhere some materials were super-resistant. They were super-conductors. Was it, Mercury that at a certain temperature lost its resistance, letting a current flow without a battery?

Ice you can predict, he thought. You can expect certain physical behaviour. But with some materials trillions and trillions of electrons coexist, coalese. They behave beyond the imagination. They don't let the magnetic field penetrate. Percy found science awe-inspiring. He thought

Nancy was radical. He thought of her heart-shaped face.

That evening he researched material and found that sometimes things happen to particles at very low temperatures. They took on this entity that no one had predicted. Nancy was one for all things quantum. She was always on about it. So now he understood about their being two things (or several things) at once.

Particles lost the magnetism but morphed and became macroscopic entity that the electrons stopped repelling. Something was happening to him he felt. It was as if his life was no longer his own.

He wondered what she was doing now. Probably reading. She did a lot of that or listening to some pod about the impediments of certain monarchs or the formation of the planet and the long march of *uncivilization* as Nancy called it. She was a robotic lawn mower.

She was a hoover…a dyson air dryer sucking up knowledge and blowing it out. He liked doing homework with her. She'd look over his shoulder and suggest this or this. And she was always laughing. Or at least very often. She'd explode with it. They'd both laugh…collapse into mirth.

Back at Lavender Gardens Nancy went over the past few days. She should have made some incendiary statement as had been her instinct but had bottled it and played the game within its stacked rules. *What a little fool she'd been,* she thought.
"Fool me once," she said out loud.

The next day a strange thing happened. Mrs Alabon, the deputy head, came in. The class sat still for this well-liked woman. She was neither young nor old, tall nor short and had a pleasing face and manner exuding confidence and approachability. Miss McBride immediately let her take the floor.

Mrs Alabon walked to Charlie and shook his hand. She nodded to Josh and then she peered around until her eyes lit on Nancy. Her expression changed and she strode across the class room stretching out a hand in congratulations. Nancy jumped up and took the proffered hand enthusiastically.

"I heard some of your suggestions from Miss McBride. I have to say I was impressed…some may even be workable," she said. Mrs Alabon returned to the front to face the class.

"Subject to parental notice being given, I intend to bring my dog into school on Friday. Nancy will you look after it during break?"

The class broke out in chatter.

"Yes," said Nancy as quick as a flash.

Mrs Alabon turned her gaze to the timetable displayed on the notice board,

"I see you have art on Friday afternoon so any objections to Erica sitting in. She's very well behaved. She settles anywhere."

The class stared at Nancy then at Mrs Alabon thinking nothing like this had ever happened before.

Nancy's shame was immediately replaced by delight. She couldn't wait to tell Percy. Amrita stroked Nancy's shoulder even though she, herself, wasn't used to dogs and was a little apprehensive.

"What sort of dog has she got?" Percy would ask.

"A Great Dane… A Harlequin! Called Erica," Nancy'd reply.
"Awesome," he'd say.

Chapter 22
Carried on Wings

Nancy considered taking her remote-controlled whoppee cushion to school. She had Mrs Truffit in her sights, who despite her rather gruff exterior Nancy considered a good egg and quite able to take a joke.

Previously Nancy had relied on this aforementioned item to visit on supply teachers' *sans merci* principally for her own amusements though it did seem to give her a cachee of sorts.

As a defence in past times, she would explain to her mother that she was conducting an experiment in human response. Her intention was to develop a face so inscrutable that one day, via the poker tables of Europe, it would make them a hoard of gold. Then there would be no defence against not having a dog. She could card count, too.

Towards the same end, Nancy had requested a lie detector for her eighth birthday and insisted her mother probed her for information.
"Nancy. Were you pleased with your present?" Fern had asked.

Nancy had been caught short. All she'd really ever hoped for as a present was a puppy.

"Mum, ask me if I've ever eaten beetroot," she redirected the conversation.

That Saturday morning, Nancy and Percy were in her garden discussing aspects of war.
"I saw a man on the news, completely blinded and with amputated hands and partially deafened by conflict who said that it wasn't his injuries that troubled him but that his country was under invasion. His wife, by his side, said she loved him even more," said Nancy.
 "The human condition," said Percy. "Don't think I'd like it."
"Sort of cool and cruel at the same time? You can see how war can generate such ambivalence. Care for a treat Percy?"
"Yes, please," he said as Nancy headed for her house.

Minutes later Nancy returned with two cones, generously filled with both Cornish and mint chocolate chip ice-cream.

"A la Aldi's…maybe not Neopolitan of the Italian riviera but pretty darn lish," she said.
"Thanks Nancy…love a chocolate chipped mint and Cornish mix!" He was never allowed such things at home.
"Oh Yesssss," said Nancy licking the ice-cream. "Mmmmint," she gasped. "Do you want to be minted?" she brushed the tip of her ice cream across Percy's face.

Annoyed, Percy jumped up off his chair. "Don't get turbulent Nancy!"
"Do you want a knuckle sandwich," Nancy mimicked and laughed and proceeded, with exaggerating licking, to devour her ice-cream.
"We going on this walk then?" she said snatching at her back pack and heading towards the back gate.

Percy would have preferred to stay in the garden but followed Nancy anyway. He was determined to relish the ice-cream even if on the hoof.
"This green, beautiful and terrible land," cried Nancy, as she held her arms out straight, like the wings of a dove. She swirled low and then high like the Wilbur brothers on a flying display. "We'll

wake this school up Percy!" she promised. "There'll be no law but our law."

Nancy was running fast. Percy didn't know if he wanted to follow at this speed but he did. Percy scrambled after her for a while and then stopped and sat down. By the time he got up to join she was out of sight. *Where have you gone?* thought Percy. He called out her name. He fastened his pace thinking she was just over the horizon but there was no sign of her. His thoughts raced.

What would have happened if they'd been in a Siberian or Russian or Afghanistan winter? He'd have got frost bite, black toes and fingers dropping off one by one never to be seen again or picked off by snipers. *She really could not be trusted. Why did he put up with this?*

All of a sudden, she leapt out at him like a Bob cat, giving him a real jolt.

"Isn't it lovely," she enthused all bright and bubbly with her orangey-red hair in perfect coordination with the green pastures. "Just glorious," she said. "Please don't forsake me," mimicked Nancy. She was still appearing very fresh. She gate-vaulted in a way he wouldn't

know where to start with even though she'd once showed him how.
"Grow up Nancy," he retaliated and plonked his coat down and sat on it. She sat down beside him in near silence. Soon all bad feeling evaporated and in rushed the tranquility of the surrounding nature. The tufts of grass, the broken-down wooden gate, the hedgerows, the sheep dung, the birds in the air. All were there, and the two of them in the middle at one with everything.

Percy felt himself lucky. The sky was blue and in that moment everything seemed to make remarkably good sense.

Nancy was lying on her back on the cool grass and he lay down beside her.
"A pop-up ice-cream business wouldn't be a bad idea. Could we rent a refrigerator at a house next to the school?" he suggested looking up at the sky.
"Perc, you're a riot," she told him. "Let the wheels of commerce roll. Overheads and profit margins…who needs a sunny disposition to get you through the bad days?" she asked.
"Yeah, I see our youthful enterprise taking on the corporate machine and it's a beautiful thing," he replied.

Things were so simple when he was with Nancy. Maybe we can all be winners after all, he thought. It was forward, forward, forward and the world didn't seem tangled up at all.

Nancy heard the sparrows who had suddenly burst in fidgety, ardent chatter. She felt it sublime to be part of a garrulous admiring group and looked back at Percy with affection.
"To be carried on wings," she marvelled. "And never have even a sniff of dark disappointment."
Percy thought her face had an intention he couldn't fathom.
"You'll have to work on not letting yourself repress yourself Percy," she said with calm conviction.
"Oh," said Percy confused to the connection between repression and suppression.
"Quite right," he followed up.
"Your mum makes a wicked smoothie," said Nancy. "And your dad when he makes bread it smells so lovely. Shall we carry on to the river?"

Percy could have laid there longer but he got up and side by side they trundled through the meadows admiring the Green Veined Whites.

"Can't beat a river trail. You'll always be on track and there's water to drink. We should go swimming." Nancy suggested.
Percy startled.
"Next time, then," said Nancy who could enjoy harmony.

Percy thought he wouldn't be telling his parents that. He, himself, wasn't at all comfortable with the idea of swimming in the river.
Sensing reluctance in her playmate, Nancy said, "We'd go in off the fishing decks,"
Still with half an eye on the water, the pair walked on, straining for the sight of a bird in the reeds or something along the riverbanks however small.
"You have to accept there are some things you can't do," said Nancy in rather preachy tones.
"But Percy this isn't one of them. There are somethings Percy that you can do but are not doing."
Percy was silent.
"I know it can be hard," she said.
They walked on.
"I'm across this," snapped Percy.
"Ah!" shrieked Nancy. "Shall we go in now?"
"No," said Percy.
"Why not?" teased Nancy.

"Don't have swimming things," said Percy.

To show both her understanding and acceptance, Nancy whistled in an exaggerated way. "Laters," she said to him with a smile and two thumbs up before leaving the subject of aggravation behind them, as an explorer might leave behind the source of a river on the way to finding its mouth. By now Percy felt both annoyed and excited, in confusingly equal measures. The two emotions see-sawed for dominance deep within his body, churning him like butter.

"Now that's the sort of positive mental attitude I can get behind," said Nancy responding to his half smile and furrowed brow.

"OMG!" she whispered to Percy in hushed amazement. "It's a Kingfisher…that is so cool."

"Where? Where?" said Percy.

"It's gone now…maybe into the bank," said Nancy.

And there they were the two children looking out at the same river but seeing different things. There were birds feeding in the next field. Percy couldn't ever remember feeling so surprised by nature. He was looking at the distant black shapes

pecking away at rich brown soil and felt a surge of fascination: an urge to venerate the crows.
"I saw a woman at Warwick castle. She had this pet crow riding around on her shoulders," said Nancy as she swung back a plait of red hair. "And I also saw a photo of this super cool woman. She was in Moscow, down in the underground station, with a live polecat riding right across her shoulder like an Edwardian Mink. Did you know Top Hats were made from Beaver fur?"
"I'd love to see that," said Percy who spoke it as if transported to the banks of the Mississippi and back through time itself. If only that were possible.
"What a lovely way to finish the week," said Nancy as they made their way home.
Percy followed her into her garden. She stopped by the rose bush, pointed and said,
"Oh, look Percy at how the white blossom lies so thickly on thorn."

Percy sat down on a yellow canvas chair. Nancy fetched some beautifully ripe cherries and joined him under the apple tree. As he put his hand into the bowl for a second cherry she watched the crimson juice drip down his jawline and saw his other hand sweep across his mouth with an easy motion.

Chapter 23
The Black Crow

On Sunday morning Nancy sat in the garden reading War and Peace and thought how much Pierre reminded her of Percy. On the table, sat watching her, was a black crow. She couldn't **ever** remember seeing a crow there before. It made a crashing sound as it flew off.

Fern and Gareth had gone out for the day. They had asked her but she hadn't fancied it. Now it was late morning and she half regretted her decision. Percy wasn't available and the day was beginning to drag. By the afternoon, she wished she'd gone too.

Nancy read, watched TV, did her homework, her Duolingo and began to study how to play Bridge. At seven o'clock in the evening her mother still wasn't back. Pangs of loneliness set in. She took a sandwich out into the garden. The sound of a dove cooing seemed to blow the wind across the garden. The sun's rays first dappled, next shadowed and then ate greedily away at the lawn, shaping it with harsh lines which threw distorted patterns and reduced the greenness of the grass.

To keep her spirits up she began to conjure various images of her dream dog. The first was a yellow dog… quite big. Not a Labrador but more a village dog. This was a familiar image, sometimes it was solid, sometimes leggy. Sometimes its fur was smooth and silky to the touch but more often it was longer and wiry. It was as if a Dingo had crossed with a Labrador. The image would morph from one mental picture to another.

The second dog was red, white and fox-like. It was smaller with a distinct patch over one eye. Its ears, again like two upright triangles, large and pricked.

Nancy was eating her sandwich and now thinking of dogs of all shapes and sizes with blue eyes, wall eyes, tails of various lengths and fur of every texture and colour. In short, dogs of every breed and mix.

A floral smell scented the air as Nancy felt a rising foreboding. Insects danced in the light around the orange umbrella. The colour matched the marching Montbretia alongside the gravelled garden path.

Then out of the blue, something strange and wonderful happened that pulled Nancy back into the here and now. She spotted in the neighbours garden a long-legged, skinny, needle-nosed whitish grey creature on the end of a rope. It was being led up the path by a middle-aged man with jeans that could not disguise his ample gut. He didn't appear the sort to be overly bothered about personal appearance. By contrast, the dog had a regal gait.

Events were rolling out fast in front of Nancy and her heartbeat quickened. Her neighbour, Mrs Pargiter had come out the back door and was on her step.

Next, she heard a gruff voice that echoed up the garden path as a clearly impatient man shouted across the cloying solitude of this Sunday evening, "She weren't my twin…this's your responsibility. You're mad at your age… shoulda let Auntie Hetties's neighbours deal with it…they were happy to have called Dogs Trust or whatever."

Carefully Mrs Pargiter took some steps down the garden; her stick tapping the ground. Previously, when seeing her neighbour Nancy had just seen a very old person. Mrs Pargiter was a figure to be avoided, if possible. She was now a person of interest.

Up till then all Nancy had seen was a stooped figure with patterned skin. She'd observed the slowness of the woman's step and been close up enough to see the deep grooves of her face, watery eyes and spindled limbs.

Once she had carried in a package and been inside. In contrast to her own home where only the bedrooms were adorned, it seemed extremely cluttered. Nancy had refused a biscuit and had entirely avoided, despite the abundance of little photo frames having to place Mrs Pargiter in a previous life or a member of any family.

So, it was on this dying evening as the sun drew in the day that a new chapter began for both these home-aloners.

Nancy watched and listened from over the fence. "Well don't expect me to help you. You're on your own there, mum. Julie thinks you're bloody mad at your age and she says she's not having a dog in the house so don't expect us to take over if you have to go into hospital or anything," said the man circling around her pulling a hesitant dog up the step into the house.

Mrs Pargiter was slowly doing an 80 degree turn and it had been clear enough that the dog and she had more to say to one another but it was difficult to judge her emotional state.

Nancy was temporarily blinded by the possibility that she should have a dog neighbour. Chemicals flew. She'd been in a street with plenty of dogs… family Labradors, spaniels, terriers, cockerpoos… dogs she could stop, pet, admire and share in the tiniest of manners but there was something wholly different in this situation. It was electrifying and Nancy, though calm under fire, was shot through (literally all over) with a series of sparkling volts.

The whole countenance of this elegant dog was no small part of this. Perhaps a greyhound, though Nancy wasn't sure, she felt it too small. Indeed, it was grey with a white band around its neck and was thin. The thin dog with long legs came up the path with a thick collar and a thin lead. It came with a man but was not a duet not a couple, not a dancing duet nor a couple of any kind. One led,

the other followed and though they were joined
by a piece of leather just inches between them,
they inhabited different worlds and one of them
had no interest in the other.

Nancy had watched them. For a moment she had
thought they were just visiting. The two of them
made an incongruous pair and Nancy supposed
the man could never let the hound off its lead.

The door closed behind them, only to reopen
quickly with the man striding forth, muttering
crossly to himself about fetching food. By his
second trip he seemed to have calmed down a
little but still held the large dog cushion thrust out
at arm's length in front of him and seemed to push
his way through the door into the kitchen.

The door closed again until minutes later the man
reappeared and was clapping his hands in front of
himself, rubbing them as if removing a sticky
mess.

"Not my responsibility," he shouted back at the
frail figure of his mother framed by the backdoor.
She knew better than to answer.

Earlier Nancy had heard him complain, "Stop meathering me." Nancy was not familiar with the term and couldn't pick up exactly how Mrs Partigiter had carried out the aforesaid meathering.

"Well if a chocolate digestive won't cheer you up I don't know what will…" she had said ignoring the fact that she had been ignored.

Nancy didn't have a plan when she walked up Mrs Pargiter's path and knocked boldly on the door.

"Come to see the dog have we?" said Mrs Pargiter who didn't look pleased to see her.

"I'm Nancy from next door."

"I know who you are…Come to see the dog have you? Never bothered before." She beckoned Nancy across the threshold.

"It were my twin's," said the elderly lady softly looking down at her slippers and tapping her stick as if to let emotion run down it.

"Never really saw what Hettie saw in it… the old Fido…doesn't seem to move."

Nancy followed Mrs Pargiter into the kitchen and saw the old dog spread out on a rug.

"Takes up half the kitchen…why couldn't she have had a nice cocker spaniel?"

"She's dead," said Mrs Pargiter. "Couldn't wait for our eighty fifth?"
"I'm sorry to hear that,"
They sat down.
"I've never been in a very mature person's house," remarked Nancy looking over at the dog.
"Ha very mature …I'm old," said Mrs Pargiter.
"I never knew my Nan," said Nancy.
"What neither one…nor your Grandads?" asked Mrs Pargiter.
"It's me and mum…and now Gareth," said Nancy.
"Yes, I like your mum. Very nice lady… Asked me to keep an eye on you. You didn't know that did ya?" she chuckled. "New fella, is he?" she continued with no hint of judgement.
"Yeah I know… I'm to come over if anything goes wrong,"
"If your house goes up in smoke just get out run," said Mrs Pargiter. "And then phone 999. Tell them I'm next door coz probably **I** won't have heard a thing." She twiddled her hearing aid and chuckled. "Can you make me a cup of tea? I don't want to trip over that … beast? Have one yourself if you fancy," she added.

In the kitchen with the kettle on the boil, the dog lying motionless, flat on its side. Nancy bent down and lightly stroked its forehead. "You have an elegant head," she stated quietly.

She ran two fingers along the length of its nose and up over its brow between its watchful eyes. The fur was softer than she had anticipated. Her fingers trailed the length of its nose, over its brow and up over the crown again and again. Slowly. Rhythmically. The dog showed no resistance. It stayed in its lying position, motionless save for a twitch of a front leg.

She flattened her palm and very gently patted it on the side of its neck.
"What's your name?" she asked it.
"Artimes…Artemisia?" she questioned in a low and steady tone.
"Her name's Queenie. My sister chose it. Will you come again tomorrow?" asked Mrs Pargiter.
Nancy nodded, adding, "Could I take her for a walk?"
"I think she'd like that," said Mrs Pargiter dunking a chocolate biscuit into her tea with a hint of a smile. But don't come til after Countdown, you can google the time," she advised more sharply.

That night a new dog appeared in Nancy's mind as she stretched out under the covers before the big yellow dog returned. The prostrate figure of this brindled-grey greyhound vyed for space with the jaunty yellow dog in all its virility and the streetwise red fox, until she fell into sleep.

**Chapter 24
Change**

Monday morning took a hand-grenade to Nancy's life.

Percy had been unavailable that weekend. It happened sometimes. Maybe the family had met up with some Uncle. Or they'd visited some exhibition. He'd phone her soon. She was dying to tell him about Mrs Pargiter and the greyhound.

"Had to go to Kew Gardens with Uncle Mick and the couzzies," or "went to the Cotswolds," he'd say half offhand, half apologetically.

Whatever the Baskervilles ever did with their weekend sounded wonderful to Nancy. Before Gareth, Nancy had thought Fern at her happiest when in Tesco's or in the back garden eating crisps with a friend. Or legs out on the foot stool, tongue out watching a soap on the sacred wall-mounted television. Nancy knew Fern's tongue didn't literally hang out but there was that marked degree of pure contentment. And now Gareth was there. Well game, set and match…unmarried bliss.

It was true Nancy was free to do what she wanted but the long Sunday afternoon left her in far from a good mood. Percy hadn't even sent a What's App. Nancy phoned. Nothing. Niente.

It must have been one of those *no phone* initiatives Mrs Baskerville had been threatening, assumed Nancy. Percy wasn't the sort to let anyone down and they always chatted on Sunday evening. It was their habit.

A cloistered Sunday often led to homework being done to a standard above and beyond. The idea of the teachers being wowed gave Nancy some satisfaction. Nancy would stay up late with an assignment that could have taken her just thirty minutes. She'd try to watch some TV with *the grown-ups* but couldn't settle and would return to the homework.

At least she'd got a visit in with Queenie but the walk had had to be quite short as the dog was just not used to it. Mrs Pargiter was prooving quite an interesting person and Nancy had mapped her life out and asked her relevant age-related questions.

There had only been one car in her street when she had been Nancy's age. It had belonged to the Draper family. Nancy now wondered if it would jeopadise her chances of seeing Queenie if she asked Mrs Pargiter to turn the TV off. It blared. Probably why Queenie preferred to stay in the kitchen.

Where was Percy? She was desperate to tell him all about this development. He was going to be amazed. She suspected he might be very good with Mrs P and as there would be two of them. Mrs P could trust them to take Queenie for long walks in the countryside. Even let her off the lead.

She would kick Percy very hard if he didn't have a good excuse for this appalling negligence. In life, sometimes a physical stand was appropriate. She still believed there would be a good reason… but the Baskervilles did have a landline and multiple devices.

Again, Nancy thought it might be some general screen time blanket ban for Sunday or something. Or they might have got back very late.

Nancy had woken that morning thinking she was to be met on the corner by Percy and his welcoming grin.

But still no message, no Percy, no meeting on the corner even though Nancy had arrived early and hung around as long as she could. As she'd stood there her mind had willed for him to come. She'd banged out texts, watching her thumbs. *Meet me on the corner.*

"Where was he? Why didn't he respond? Should she wait or should she not wait. Should she go on to school?"

Nancy felt disorientated as she finally walked to school on her own. Her heart slowly spiralling downwards like a doodlebug with wings aflame.

He wasn't in the playground when she arrived on time by the skin of her teeth. Register dragged. Assembly dragged.

 A nonchalant Percy, his shoulders sloped, would come into school, imagined Nancy. She hoped. The morning dragged. Nancy felt increasingly uneasy. Everything seemed out of step.

Register, Maths, English…

At break she braved interrupting the football game to ask Josh if he'd heard anything from Percy. A boy, who'd Nancy never spoken to, overheard her asking and called across the playground, "He's moving today. They're off to America…you should see the removal lorry. It's enormous."

Noah stopped the ball, picked it up and started bouncing it with his toe, counting.
"What? Is Percy moving?" he said.
"Looks that way," said William.
"Wow I'd love to move to America," said Lucas.
"Nah…they don't play proper football. They call this soccer. Pass it here Noah!"
There was this slow crash, Nancy's doodle bug. It crashed burning, flashing blindingly brightly.

The bell went. *For whom the bell tolls.* She felt her world blur…or rather that she was now sat outside of it. She was the drone hovering, suspended.
"Now today we will learn about grid references," she heard Miss McBride say.
"Just Google map it, Miss?" called out Josh and the class laughed.

It was ten minutes before the lunch bell when there was a knock on the classroom door and in came Percy.

"I'm sorry for not waiting til lunch Miss but Mum says we have to leave for the airport. I've come to collect my things and say goodbye," he said.

"Ah. Yes, Percy. But shouldn't you be in Year 6," said Miss McBride.

"Yeah, yeah…I'll go there next," he said.

"Class 5 can we all give Percy a warm goodbye and good luck?"

A chorus of goodbyes crisscrossed the airwaves.

"I had no idea you were going…Are you coming back?" said Miss McBride.

Percy dropped his head. The class kept on shouting out, "Good luck," and "*Bon* Voyage". It was all very spirited.

Percy pulled out something from his bag. A card and said something.

Miss McBride felt she was losing control of Year 5. "You get off to Year 6 before the lunch bell," she urged. "I'll see to this," taking the card from his hand.

Percy found Nancy sitting alone in the playground. She had the card with her. Percy sat down beside her.

"They only told me on Friday. I wanted to tell you in person," he said gently. "They wouldn't let me come around on Friday. We had to go and see the Uncles."
Nancy just stared out in front of her.
"Ada's been screaming."
She gave a faint turn of the head.
"Where and for how long?"
"North Carolina. Five years."
A bullet went through her.
"Mum's work contract,"
The bullet shattered.
"We can still keep in touch."
Nancy nodded.
She patted him on the knee and said, "I know…"
He looked at his knee and then at her.
Through two lips, parted in a perfect circle, she whispered, "I'll miss you *Perch*."
Silence was loading again when Percy said,
"I gotta go now…"
Nancy said nothing.
"They're waiting outside. It's a taxi," said Percy.

It was a sad farewell. The sky hung dark over the hills of the village.
Nancy just couldn't look up.

Epilogue

July settled in and the summer
holidays began to raise its head with two pointed ears pricking up over the canopy.

The teachers, although exhausted and a bit miserable, managed by the middle of the penultimate week to crack a smile. A certain spring in their step was perceived by Nancy.

There were the usual mumblings of reports but altogether there was a more cheerful tone to the school day. There was the school trip.

She sat by Amrita on the way back from Compton Verney. After sharing some friendly banter both girls opened books. Nancy couldn't concentrate as, in her mind's eye sat Percy.
"If you were to have the perfect dog what would it be?" she asked him.
Percy smiled and said, "Pug" and they both burst out laughing.
"That is so mean to Pugs," she told him, offering him a fig roll.

On the last day of term, Nancy remained behind in the classroom. Miss McBride stopped what she was doing and asked, "Most amazing River, Nancy?"
Nancy shrugged.
"Longest Nile. Biggest Amazon," she said flatly.

Then Miss McBride detected a slight change in Nancy so imperceptible it was like a feather touch and Nancy said, "Though like much in this life, it depends on who tells you. Depends on who you ask. I read the Amazon has five times the output of the Congo but the Congo at its deepest is 720 metres deep."

Nancy lifted her gaze and set it on Miss McBride and said, "But, it's not the length, nor the width and depth. It's the force of its flow."

Miss McBride looked down and then up and knew she must part with Harvey.
"So Nancy, the Summer holidays are here. Any plans?" she asked.

"I shall walk in circles. Read from oblongs. And love in a triangle," said Nancy.
"Love in a triangle Nancy?" said Miss McBride.

"Why, yes, Miss McBride, eight legs are better than two," said Nancy and left Miss McBride in the classroom.

Miss McBride was making plans to have eight legs: a man and twins and of course her own two to run around after them.

For the last time that summer, Nancy made her way across the playground, seeing Percy in each corner and remembered their fun-soaked walks home together.

Once out of the school gates, Nancy turned left. Instantaneously up her heart lifted, as there was Fern, leaning against a lamp post, holding a long lead and on its end was Queenie whose tail was gently wagging.

Tribute

Flush by **Virginia Woolf**

And as he lay there, exiled, on the carpet, he went through one of those whirlpools of tumultuous emotion in which the soul is either dashed upon the rocks and splintered or, finding some tuft of foothold, slowly and painfully pulls itself up, regains dry land, and at last emerges on top of a ruined universe to survey a world created afresh on a different plan. Which was it to be – destruction or reconstruction.

Printed in Dunstable, United Kingdom